Our Shadows Never Die
Stories
By
Andy Slade

This is a work of fiction. Similarities to real people, places, or events are entirely coincidental.

OUR SHADOWS NEVER DIE

First edition. December 1, 2023.

ISBN: 979-8223851318

Written by Andy Slade.

Also by Andy Slade

Betrayal Is Beautiful
Our Shadows Never Die

Table of Contents

The Rest 1

Far Cries...3

The Many Apologies of Orville Carmody.............................5

The Anniversary Party 11

Dead Husband Money 21

The Migrants: A Photo Album..29

Are We a Thing? 31

Microboy Never Loved Christina 34

The Coat on the Chair 59

The Sound of Shadows 72

Tony's Last Grandma 81

Music for Simana...91

Greed Doesn't Count 93

The Rest

"**R**est awhile," was all she said to me as my daily journey ended. She patted the concrete ledge under the I-40 overpass on 12th St.

I'd made the trip in no time. Usually, when the summer heat blasted hard like it always did in Albuquerque — and today was like always — I would walk from shade to shade. So, I rested.

"Where you from?" she asked.

"No place in particular."

I was too tired to talk anymore. Leaning back, I felt the heavy vehicles pass by overhead, but I felt safe. When I woke up, she was gone. She looked like someone's mother, maybe mine. I wasn't sure who I looked like because I hadn't seen myself in a while.

Always wait until it's dark was how I was taught to travel. If you wait and look, you might make it. If you listen to others, you might learn where it's safe to go, but it's a choice, and you know how choices can be.

I found myself in the city shelter eating dry ramen and moldy Oreos left on a vacant cot. I asked around—one or two people because asking too much can get you into trouble—if they'd seen the nice lady. A tall old man, thin with large bony hands with swollen knuckles, who was bent over even when he tried to walk, asked me if I knew that he'd recently won an oil well by eating an Oreo. I said no; I hadn't. He started crying over nothing and made me feel bad.

I decided today I would travel in the morning. When I walked away into the sunlight, I asked a skateboarding standalone if he had seen the nice lady that slept under overpasses; he took out his earphones and said he couldn't hear me and even if he did, he wouldn't talk to a fucked up kid that lived on the street. I didn't exactly thank him, but I should have because he looked cool.

I could never tell what time it was, but I could tell how long it had been; too long or not very long, or just about right was all I could tell. When I found her, it had been too long and I could tell she didn't remember me right off. She was shooting up inside the dumpster behind the Waffle House on Zuni.

I told her not to worry too much, and that everything was going to be OK as I pulled the needle out of her dead arm and cried a prayer for her. After that, I ate some fresh dumpster hash browns. They were still warm.

I told her to rest awhile. She couldn't listen anymore. I closed the dumpster lid on us and stayed with her for a while. Then I left, closed the lid as softly as I could and kissed it, keeping the memory of her kindness with me for all my journeys to come.

C rescent Mahoney lived in the middle of a Moon Pie. It had always been Pops, herself, and Mama. Mama would always say, "Wait a minute! Before you go, call me."

Mama Mahoney could cry on demand; it came to her as easy as her loneliness. Everything was Breaking News. Headlines now, details later. Details like, I love you, later, as her brittle Polaroids faded into irrelevance. They were somewhere, but she couldn't remember.

Pops Mahoney decided many years ago to direct his anger at the world by drinking more and more until he couldn't feel a thing. "You don't have to call me, OK?" Alright, it doesn't matter.

• • • •

CRESCENT CAUGHT HER illusion on a selfie yesterday: Agnes, the Big Mistake, smiled at her over her shoulder and blew her a kiss with two fingers from in front of her mouth. A cup of coffee might make everything right. So Crescent went to their little kitchen and brewed a cup.

She could feel her hand trembling as she watched the ripples in her cup of coffee. They were as quiet as forgotten dreams. She followed them carefully to see where they went. They never returned. Tiny bubbles lapped at the edge and popped. Going nowhere seemed about right.

Pops told her he had a little liver cancer, and it was no big deal and he'd be fine, but right now, he was going fishing. He'd been trying to catch 'Big Whiskers' for many years now and he was surer than ever that today was the day. Pops claimed that 'Big Whiskers' could read minds, so he had to put his intentions out of his mind and just let things happen.

• • • •

IT WAS NOW THE BIG Squeeze inside The Moon Pie. Agnes, Crescent's 'partner in crime', could see her checking out, but there was nothing she could do. Pops called Agnes 'Your partner in crime' because he didn't have the strength to deal with any of it, not that Crescent could blame him. After all, she was dealing with it herself. Solitaire should only be played in a locked room by yourself with a dirty light bulb hanging over your head. Agnes told Crescent to shut up and deal.

Mama called Crescent tomorrow because that's when today leaves and never comes back. It's when Mama would cry her last love poem to Pops from a place so far away that even God couldn't hear it. He probably had better things to do, anyway.

The Many Apologies of Orville Carmody

THE PROMISE OF TOMORROW
I cannot promise you tomorrow
For that is up to you.
Dream of it
And it is yours,
Live it with all your heart,
Live all your tomorrows
Today,
In the Light of Hope,
Along the way.
Orville Carmody

• • • •

THERE WAS A POEM THAT came to Orville Carmody while he was deep in thought. He cared little for this 'red-headed stepchild', because it irritated him and he didn't know why.

To him, his poems were his children, but there were too many of them to keep. Some had to be sent away. He would forward them to poetry magazines to see if someone would care for them. They remained homeless.

He often thought about his children. For instance, he thought, where were they now? What had happened to them? Soon after, a heartfelt apology to them would always follow.

• • • •

HE LIVED AT THE MALPAIS Retirement Community of Rio Rancho, where he wrote his poetry in the afternoon sunlight. So radiant, so perfect, so beautiful!

His face belied its years, and there was a profound peace in his barely noticeable, ever-present smile. Youthful optimism sculpted his face. Time's relentless erosions were thwarted by his intense love of the world around him.

He was a frail-looking man, slightly stooped in posture, thinner than most men, and no taller than five feet one or two. His wispy hair was thin and gray, but his eyes told a different story. They were young, crystal blue, and electric!

He retired as a Senior Clerk 4 from the local Social Security Office in Albuquerque. "The Little Hermit", as he was called by his ex-colleagues, could have gone further up the ladder, but he couldn't bear the thought of hindering someone else's progress. His attention to detail about his daily habits and duties was his way of life. But, above all else, he was a dreamer.

Orville thought best at night. He thought while he dusted his modest furniture with an old handkerchief he kept in his back pants pocket. After he dusted, he would open his front door as quietly as possible and gently shake off the dust free. It wasn't necessary, but he always offered a modest apology to any creature out there that he might have offended by his actions.

Everything he did was clean and inoffensive, like the clothes he wore. Orville wasn't like the other residents, as all he wanted was to be left alone to write. You couldn't tell if anyone lived in his apartment except for the occasional sound of his old T.V. broadcasting the local news.

• • • •

A STRUGGLING ATLANTA-based poetry journal called 'No Time' had barely survived the previous twelve years. There had been too many years of thin advertising revenue and minor subscription fees. When the owner died, he left it to anyone willing to take it on.

Enter Ted Gold. The balding, fortyish, overweight, and not averse to feeling sorry for himself staff editor, reluctantly raised his hand. He'd grown tired of being broke and taking orders from everyone.

This was an opportunity he couldn't pass up, a new life for himself, maybe. So Ted changed everything, including his personal appearance. He knew the business had to change. It needed a purpose for living.

He fired everyone that needed firing.

He shredded the archives, except for one poem.

One night, he woke up drenched in sweat. At first, he thought it was the June heat wave hitting Atlanta, but then he realized it wasn't the heat at all. It was his newfound treasure! He didn't know what to do with it.

Then, like being hit by a bolt of lightning, everything came together. The title of the poem was 'The Promise of Tomorrow'. That was it! His new marketing campaign!

. . . .

IT WAS A TOUGH TIME for Retirement Communities across the country, and Malpais was no exception. There were too many empty chairs and the steep drop in revenue was disturbing. Malpais needed help. Ted Gold showed up and told them he was their answer. He used social media hacks and slick messages of hope to get the lucrative marketing contract.

When the ad campaign came out and the catchy poem caught the public's attention, specifically the back end of the Boomer population, requests to live at Malpais poured in.

Once again, as with other Retirement Communities hearing Ted's promise, the poem connected with many of the senior citizens as they battled old age at Malpais. It didn't matter if you were a lover of poetry; the words went down like warm honey. The empty chairs were getting filled. Everything seemed to be fine until that Sunday morning.

. . . .

HIS FOCUS ON THE LUCRATIVE contract at Malpais required his personal touch, which, for Ted, meant visiting and speaking to the residents. He walked around, meeting with them and shaking their fragile, bony hands.

Breakfast in the dining room was the perfect place for his presentation. Everyone was friendly, including Orville Carmody, who paid little attention to any of it until the presentation ended. After Ted explained his marketing campaign, the residents ate their scrambled eggs and oatmeal, just like always.

It was time for the Morning Prayer and sermon. A local preacher, Reverend Felix Foster, who regularly gave generic sermons to the residents on Sunday mornings, ended his sermon by reciting the poem that had brought new life to their community.

After he made sure that he'd gotten everyone's attention, he cited the words of hope as coming directly from God. Sitting at the dais just behind the preacher, Ted nodded his head enthusiastically as the recitation began. The applause was generous, especially from the newer residents.

When the applause ended, something unexpected happened. Apparently, Orville lost his mind. He stood up and yelled, "Thief!" He pointed directly and emphatically at God. "Thief!"

Everyone's eyes followed Orville as he made his way up to the preacher. A few of them shook their heads, as older adults often do when one of them makes a dumb but excusable comment. Some residents left to avoid embarrassment.

"Why do you defame our Lord with such a sacrilege?" asked the preacher.

"You said the words came from God."

Laura McGinnis, the Administrator, walked up to the preacher in case she had to intervene when Orville approached him. One of her responsibilities was to smooth over the sometimes-abrasive comments made by residents. This instance was right in her wheelhouse.

"Mr. Carmody, sometimes, well, we think things are one way, but we soon realize that they aren't," said the Administrator. "It's one of those things that happens to us as we age. It's quite normal, really. I'm sure the poem rang a bell with you because it is so beautiful and you took the words into your heart. That's all. I'm certain of that."

"I didn't take them into my heart."

"I'm not sure I understand."

"It's quite simple Laura. The words were already there."

The preacher gave a muted confession.

"Mr. Carmody, I think I understand. You are questioning whether the words came from God. All words come from God. The words live in His Glory. That's all I was saying. It has given hope, or a new beginning, you might say."

Orville had heard enough and left.

• • • •

THE REASON HE WROTE the letter to Ted Gold shortly after the dust up in the dining room was unknown. But in it, he asked why Ted had stolen his poem and why was he using it to make money. Unfortunately, Ted never responded.

A month later, after many thoughts, he wrote another letter to Ted as a poem, a poem of apology. He asked Ted to forgive him for his rudeness in the previous letter. He told him that the words were for anyone who wanted them. Again, there was no response from Ted.

• • • •

LAURA VISITED ORVILLE on a sunny afternoon in September, as she wanted to see how he was getting along. The sunlight piercing through his window was brilliant and beautiful. It had warmth and clarity, more so than she'd ever noticed before. This was his afternoon light of inspiration.

She wanted to know why he gave up on his battle to reclaim his poem. After all, it was his. He showed her a copy he'd kept of the original, like a parent showing a photograph of their child to friend. After he had initially claimed the poem as his, she never doubted his claim from that point on.

Her wry smile revealed she knew what he'd say when she asked him the question. "Do you know you could have become wealthy if you proved your ownership of the poem?"

"Well, it's like this Laura. Good words are words that move us. We all have words that are special to us. Don't we?" He paused for a few seconds. "You know, Laura, hope is a rare commodity these days." He pointed with an open palm at the sunlight streaming through the window. "I get mine from my teacher."

It was now time for her to leave. "Don't get up Orville. Stay where you are. It's OK."

He tried his hardest, but he couldn't get up. He apologized for his discourtesy, asked for her forgiveness, and graciously thanked her for her visit.

• • • •

ORVILLE CARMODY HAD no living relatives, except, of course, for his 'children'. To ensure his 'child' stayed with him along the way, Laura had his love poem to the world carved prominently on his headstone.

And even though Ted Gold disputed Orville's authorship of the poem with a weak legal action, Laura recommended strongly to him he drop the suit and just let the words themselves carry their own message. He never once said that he'd stolen the poem, but then again, he didn't pursue further legal action either. Perhaps the words meant more to him than he would admit.

Orville would have understood.

The Anniversary Party

James Cullen MacDonald loved his wife, Mary Eunice MacDonald, more than life itself. One unfortunate day, Mary lost her mind at the Grand Mall in Far Rockaway. Jimmy spent the rest of his life looking for it, in case Mary wanted it back one day.

What I'm about to relay to you, the reader of this tale of true love, are the facts as they happened.

And if you find some interest in this story, my advice to you is the same for this or any other story of true love. Do not be swayed by facts.

• • • •

IT WAS ON AN EARLY Thursday morning in Far Rockaway, late in October, that Jimmy lost his own mind, but there was no one around to help him find it. Jimmy and Mary had no children, even though Mary occasionally would say she wanted children. When you're eighty-eight like Jimmy was and pissed off at the world, the reasons don't matter very much. He knew he was losing his wife, and that was enough.

According to his watch, it was 5:48 a.m. Two long shadows slid along the moonlit sand at the end of Beach 27th Street, Jimmy's street. They took their orders directly from the moon and grew longer and thinner like stilettos, piercing the approaching dawn. October mornings in Far Rockaway can freeze your soul, if you let them. Jimmy didn't have to give permission. The imminent demise of his soul had already been in the works because Mary wouldn't be around much longer.

• • • •

MOST OF THE RESIDENTS in Far Rockaway were still sleeping when Jimmy started counting the waves on the beach. He noticed the shadows before, but they had vanished.

"Can you see the old son-of-a-bitch yet?" asked the red-haired, lanky one.

"No, not yet, but we better do this before the sun comes up," whispered his partner.

The two thirteen-year-olds crouched behind a boulder. They each held hand-sized rocks ready to launch at Jimmy sitting on his porch, looking through his WWII binoculars.

"You go first," said Stuey Feldman, "then I'll go." His red hair was standing straight up.

Alex Kyler, one of the neighbor kids, stood up slowly and yelled loud enough to be heard by the old man. "Hey Jimmy, seen anything good this morning?"

He threw the rock, and it shattered the living room window behind the old man, covering Jimmy in glass. The second rock missed everything. Their scattering footsteps reminded him of vermin in dark places.

"That you, Alex?" Jimmy's weak voice didn't project. "No matter." Jimmy resumed his counting. "Eighteen..." he forgot where he was, so he began counting again. He was counting waves through his binoculars again. He focused the lenses on the gritty sand on the beach. It looked brown, and the waves made small bubbles, coming and going. He could smell the ocean from his porch and kept counting. He lip-synced their rhythm.

His Mary was dying. He just found out last week. No matter what he'd ever done, it never mattered to her. She just put up with his 'ways'. He thought about the kids who threw the rocks. He'd done the same thing many times as a little punk and never thought twice about it.

If you know how many there are of something, you can get to know them better. It's how you get to the heart of them. For instance, two kids and a hundred waves. Two and One Hundred. Two and One Hundred. Two and... What about heartbeats? They said he was a 'Peeping Tom', because he was always looking through his binoculars.

As he counted more waves, he moved his binoculars down to the street in front of his house. He couldn't believe his eyes. His long-dead father, Paddy MacDonald, was standing right there.

"Again, you son-of-a-bitch?" yelled Jimmy at the top of his lungs. His voice was powerful now.

And there he was, Patrick 'Paddy' MacDonald, his father, carrying that old brown suitcase, the one with the rope tied around it to keep it together. He was running away all over again. And there was Ginny Sloan, smoking that same damn cigarette and smiling that same big wide smile. It was a big hole in her face with a dark red outline that was supposed to make her look pretty.

Paddy threw his suitcase in the back of the Dodge and started the engine, but it wouldn't start.

He tried again and nothing. Paddy looked around the neighborhood and turned the key again, but the groaning ignition produced nothing. On the fourth try, the engine finally turned over. Ginny kept smiling through that hole in her face. She threw her arms around Paddy, pressing everything she had on him in case he thought about changing his mind. To make it official, they signed their exit in a swirl of blue green exhaust and a loud cracking backfire.

The kids at school drew a big red heart on the schoolyard cement and in the middle of it was written, 'Paddy and Ginny Forever'.

Ginny's son Danny didn't go to school that day. But he waited for Jimmy after school the next day. He blamed Jimmy and his father for losing his mother. Jimmy liked to fight, but he didn't have it in him that day as there was nothing to fight for. You gotta have something to fight for. It was the least he could do for Danny to let him win. He swore he'd never do that again, even though he did.

Jimmy's dear mother, Bertie, lost her will to live. She was never the same after Paddy left. God rest her soul.

Jimmy left school and took odd jobs to put food on the table. His mother Bertie's loneliness and pain never stopped, no matter what he did.

When she died, Jimmy buried her, but no one came to the funeral.

There were other funerals that day. He could see everyone in their long black coats.

When the Portareekin gravediggers put Bertie deep in the ground, one of them, the older and heavier one with the gray mustache, whispered something loud enough to his partner so Jimmy could hear it, and they both laughed.

They looked at Jimmy as if Bertie didn't deserve her grave. On any other day, he would have beaten the living shit out of both of 'em, especially when they stuck their hands out for a tip. But that day belonged to Bertie. So he took a deep breath and said goodbye. When he left, they knocked over her headstone.

His watch read 7:25. He shook it and put it to his ear. It was time to check on Mary again. As he stood up, he dropped his binoculars and shed broken window pieces in a soft shower of crystal rain.

The lenses of his binoculars fractured.

• • • •

MORNINGS ALWAYS BELONGED to Mary. Jimmy struggled, but he always gave her a sponge bath and straightened her bedding. She was cold, so he apologized to her and put two blankets on her as he kissed her cheek.

There was a deep and endless sadness in him.

• • • •

WHEN BERTIE PASSED away, in that same room, he never forgave himself. He'd been working that day and, as usual, he was too busy stirring up shit. Isn't that what union thugs are supposed to do? Damn right it is!

That kind of work came naturally to Jimmy just like using his fists, whipping skulls with his pistol, pissing people off, and drinking too much. A million times or more, he told Bertie that Paddy left because of him, not her.

He had nothing to say when he came home from work and found his mother had passed. Her mouth was wide open, like she was about to say something before she passed away. For Bertie, dying was a better option because according to her, words were bullshit. And, of course, she was right. She was always right.

But now, he gently touched Mary's arm, in case she needed to know he was there. He thought he had caught a smile on her face. Like always, he left her love notes with his eyes.

Jimmy was about to leave when he noticed the calendar on the wall. A faded circle drawn around January 27 reminded him that their anniversary was coming up. The calendar was from 1976. He'd left it there because it was Mary's last good year.

Most people thought Jimmy MacDonald was an asshole, and maybe he was, but she loved him anyway because she knew he wasn't and that was good enough for the both of them.

For a minute, he couldn't remember where he was. He stood in the hallway, scratching his head. Then he remembered he had to find his good suit. He found it in the hanging vinyl storage bag with the zipper all around and the mothballs inside.

The smell of camphor, and the rustling of Mary's special dress—the long blue and white one she kept for special occasions—were all inside, arranged by Mary. The dress still had a faded white rose pinned to it. In the bag, he found his dark brown suit and his black patent leather shoes.

He closed his eyes, took in a deep breath, and gave his memory a chance to catch up. His marine uniform was there, with the shoes, his Commendation for Bravery under Fire, his old gun and the bright red tie he bought for their wedding.

• • • •

JIMMY BEGAN THE CLEANUP, starting with the front yard and the porch. Then he found a note attached to his front door. It was posted by the Beach 27th St. Neighborhood Association and it pissed him off.

It read: "The current conditions of your residence represent a hazard to the public. You have ten days to repair/correct these conditions or legal action will be taken."

He folded the note slowly and pushed it deep into his pants pocket as far down as possible. Then he looked around the neighborhood with a big grin on his face.

There wasn't much time left for him to get everything arranged. Mary always liked things just so. He had the front window replaced. Everything had to be done right, so he spent the next two days shopping for food, getting artificial roses and cleaning up the house.

The 'new' Jimmy wore new clothes, shaved, got a haircut, and smiled. He could hear Mary's voice now, telling him she knew he could do it, especially when he would 'talk nice' to people.

The big question in the neighborhood was, 'Who was this guy?' No one could figure it out. Some people said he found God and was getting ready to meet his maker. A few others shrugged it off and ignored the old bastard altogether.

He couldn't recall if the fence in front had been white, but he painted it white, anyway, as Mary liked white. When he saw Elaine Kline picking up trash in her front yard, he even waved at her.

"I want you and Izzy to come to our sixtieth wedding anniversary on Tuesday. Mary and I would both love to have you come over. I've put an invitation in your mailbox and the Bernstein's box. It's for Mary, mostly. She's not been feeling well lately, you know, and she asked me to invite you."

She couldn't believe what she was hearing. That old man never once talked to her in all the years they lived there, and as for Mary, no one could remember when they'd last seen her. What was he up to?

The old man even removed his cap while he spoke, to soften his words. "Oh, and she has very special gifts for all of you. It's something you'll treasure for the rest of your life."

"Don't know if we can make it, but we'll check it out and let you know." Elaine Kline hurried back inside her house, glancing back over her shoulder at the reinvented troublemaker.

• • • •

THE BIG DAY HAD ARRIVED, and he took a break. The porch chair creaked as he sat down. He couldn't feel his big hammer hands as they'd been numbed by the freezing air.

Maybe they weren't his hands after all. How could they be? How many times had he used them on the streets and the docks? If they hit you, you stayed hit. When he was young, he never wore gloves in the cold weather like all the other pussies who talked big but couldn't handle shit.

Even the sun froze behind the clouds. Too cold, he guessed. Then he remembered he hadn't counted his waves yet, so he groped around for his binoculars and found them just where he'd dropped them earlier, shattered lenses and all. Funny, he didn't remember.

He'd never seen these waves before; the waves appeared in pieces, fractured, and more beautiful than before.

It made him remember his sixth birthday. Bertie had given little Jimmy a kaleidoscope, and when he looked into it and turned it, he couldn't get enough of what he saw. He liked what he saw so much that he really wished it were real. When you're a kid, you can wish like that. When you're old, it's a waste of time, unless... Well, suppose you knew...

• • • •

WHEN THE TIME ARRIVED for the Party to start, his guests showed up. He knew they'd come.

Jimmy, the 'new' Jimmy, was wearing his good suit. Mary was also in her special dress. The clock on the wall said 5:55 p.m. when he wheeled Mary to her place. She would sit to his right at the dining room table. As he lit the two candles, the doorbell rang. He graciously greeted the Klines and the Bernsteins and escorted them into his house.

"Welcome, welcome, welcome, be seated." He seemed a little rushed, but they were glad to get it over with.

"Your names are written on cards. Mary likes everything to be formal like this, so if you don't mind." Jimmy opened his palm and pointed at the table. "I know how busy you are, and Mary is very weak, so please sit so we can start."

The Klines, Izzie and Elaine, and the Bernsteins, Maury and Rose, looked at each other and sat slowly in their places. No one said a word.

He asked if they were comfortable, but no one responded as he attempted to push in the chairs for the ladies, but they did it themselves.

And finally, he sat down at the head of the table with Mary on his right and Elaine Kline on his left. Before the meal started, he raised his glass of wine and proposed a toast.

"Please, everyone. I want to make a toast to the most wonderful woman I've ever known. She's been with me all these years, through thick and thin, always there for me, and always doing her best even when I made her life miserable. But, somehow, mostly thanks to her, we made it through all of that. So, here's to you, Mary."

They all lifted their glasses and drank their wine.

"Thank you," said Jimmy.

Almost instantaneously, Jimmy suddenly pulled out a pistol and shot Mary in her head. He did it at such close range that the powder burns could be seen. He immediately pointed the gun at Elaine Kline's head. The trigger was cocked.

"No one move or she's next."

Fear and Jimmy's shaking hand brought everyone to attention. Then he continued his speech.

"I hope you will enjoy this very special meal. I've worked on it all day to make sure it's perfect for you. See, I know I haven't been a very good neighbor all these years, but it doesn't mean I don't appreciate you. After all, you can't help being who you were or are, can you? For instance, you, Rose, you couldn't help being who you were when you brought your lover into your house when your husband went on his business trip back in '78. Or you, Izzie, you couldn't help it when your wife went to visit her sick and dying mother back in '67 and you and your friends brought in those hookers for that night of fun?"

The guests had nothing to say as Jimmy recounted what he'd witnessed over the years. He rattled off a few more incidents and said, "Well, that's enough. It's time to open your gifts. Please." They opened their gifts, finding loaded and cocked guns inside each box. "Now, please remove the gun and point it directly at me, if you don't mind." They hesitated to do so, making Jimmy irritated. "No, please pick them up now." Jimmy waved his own gun closer to Elaine's head and insisted, so they complied.

"Ok, now please point your weapons at me and when I count down to one, I want you to shoot. Don't try anything stupid or I'll shoot Elaine. Oh, and by the way, if you like, you can shoot me between now and one."

Maury tried to intervene. "Look MacDonald, don't do this."

"Ten, nine, eight, seven,.." said Jimmy. No one moved a muscle. "Six, five, four, three..."

Maury and Izzy shot and killed Jimmy to save Elaine.

• • • •

THEY BECAME KNOWN AS 'The Firing Squad' after the Medical Examiner had determined that Mary MacDonald had been dead for approximately twenty-four hours before Jimmy shot her. Their appeal went nowhere and their first degree murder verdict of guilty, stood.

A letter arrived at both homes of the 'Firing Squad'. It was neatly typed by Jimmy, but I won't print it here. It thanked both families for helping him through his difficult situation and wished them well in their future life endeavors: life without the possibility of parole.

Dead Husband Money

"*There are only three kinds of money in Hollywood: Decent money, Dead Husband money, and Warren Grant money and none of them will buy you anything but trouble.*" - Anonymous

• • • •

THE ONLY WAY HE COULD see through this kind of LA fog was to close his eyes, which was also the best way to handle the impossible, like believing that he, the great Cotton Palmer, loved Gloria Stewart, the wife of the late character actor, Brian Stewart.

He sat motionless in his car, opened his tired eyes and watched the slapping wipers temporarily remove the fog and slow drizzle from his cracked windshield.

He couldn't help but remember the argument they'd had years before in the parking lot of Slammin' Joe's, the gin dump just outside of Burbank. No one saw him in the fog as he scuffled with Brian Stewart, who eventually died after falling and hitting his head on a rock. Cotton left him there.

This was the same fog. Everyone knew he was the better actor, everyone. He took another drink from his gold-plated flask and placed it next to the two-grand from Gloria. If you bothered to look, you could see the sticker on the bottom of the flask that read, 'Property of Goldman Studios'. The two-grand was enough for now; she had plenty.

• • • •

THERE WAS A GOOD REASON Cotton Palmer was an alcoholic. However, it wasn't one of those familiar reasons, like insecurity, self-loathing or any other crap like that. His reason was as clear as the gin he swilled every time he thought about it.

21

He'd grown up in Hollywood, got work in Hollywood, went through the cycle in Hollywood, and when his cycle ended, Hollywood embraced him for what he was.

• • • •

IN 1922, HIS MOTHER Carolyn got divorced and drove from Indiana to Hollywood, not for fame or fortune but for the sun and the warmth. Palmer had been a well-behaved child, but when Carolyn passed away at thirty-seven, he went hard into survival mode and into the motion picture industry. He gaffed, broke down sets, and even took prat falls as an extra, falling on cue.

He had enough looks to get a few character parts. His face was 'interesting' but not enough to make real money. Along the way, he learned how to drink. But his acting was different.

Even though there was a method to his madness, there was none in his acting. His acting was all Cotton Palmer. In fact, other serious actors took notice of how good he really was. He was so good, in fact, that hiring him became mandatory if you wanted to make the film believable. If they couldn't get him for a supporting role, which was usually the Heavy, they would hold out until the studio hired him. That's when he started making decent money.

As he approached the age of forty-five, he realized he would never be recognized for his talent or the art he brought to his talent. If the studios wouldn't appreciate what he had and pay him for it, maybe life would.

He could stab you in your back, throw you to a wolf, or kiss your ass. His free-time activities included playing the ponies and bilking dowagers out of their dead husband's money. Dead husband money came easy, and it always came gift-wrapped.

But after eleven years in that role, he woke up one day and decided he wanted roles in films. Time was pushing him into a corner.

He trolled the studios, literally begging for any part he could get. Some producers even turned it into a game by pretending to listen and that's how it went.

. . . .

AMONG THE MANY LISTS in the film industry, the-List was always full, because it's very short. Warren Grant had been at or near the top of it for almost twenty years. His face was a masterpiece that made love to his audience, who were unanimous in their worship of him. Women loved him and men admired him. His skill as an actor was decent enough, but for insurance, he always surrounded himself with the best supporting actors, technical people, cameramen and top-flight directors. He could command those players whenever he needed them. He had options on all the popular novels of the day, so it was easy to get a built-in audience ready to pay.

In the past, whenever he could get him, Grant almost always asked for Cotton Palmer. But like most A-Listers, Warren Grant and his money were inseparable. He paid his supporting team next to nothing. His fans didn't care, because even they knew that greed doesn't count.

In the 1950s, Grant became a full-time producer. It was a simple transition, moving from star to producer, since he was always in charge of every aspect of his films, anyway. He didn't care about being a star as long as the big money was there for him, and it was. Getting has-beens for a song was his stock in trade. All of them, including Zena Powell, hated his song and his guts.

Zena and Cotton hadn't seen each other for years. They had worked together on a few films in the thirties, when Zena was beautiful but on-the-fade, and Cotton was just starting out his career. It was said that they were an item back then, but no one knew for sure. She kept her toe in the water after she retired, got occasional T.V. roles, and lived her retirement years in comfortable anonymity. That was until she heard that knock, that fateful knock at her front door.

When she opened the door and saw Cotton Palmer, that well-practiced frown of skepticism greeted her old protégé.

"Zena, love, how can you greet an old friend like that?"

"For you Cotton, it's the only way, and you're not my old friend."

"Not very nice, dear," said Palmer as he edged his way into the dusty remnants of her faded career. The dust covered everything but floated like gold dust for Mr. Down-And-Out. "Actually, I was lonely, and you were the first person I thought about."

"How much?" asked Zena.

He pregnant-paused his angst. "Very hurtful, love. And what do you mean exactly by 'how much'?"

"It means what it's always meant. How much money do you want from me to get you the hell out of my life?"

"I can't believe you'd say something like that."

"How much? That's all I want to know," asked Zena.

"Two hundred and I swear I'll pay you back as soon as..."

"Two hundred? Are you kidding me?" Zena overacted a bit and let her mouth open too much. "I don't have that kind of money. Besides, I wouldn't give it to you if I did."

"I'm only asking because it's been a little dicey out here lately in the real world and..."

"I've got a better idea. Instead of money, I'll give you something better."

"Like what?"

"Like a job."

"What job?"

"Paradise Studios is filming 'Cargo', the life of Manley Thomas, the spy who sold our missile sites to the Chinese. Warren Grant needs someone to play Parnell Gray, the double agent ex-best friend runner, who delivers the cash to Manley. It's only two, maybe three minutes on screen, but it's credited. Grant called me this morning and asked me if I knew anyone who'd fit the role. I told him no, but I actually think you'd fit it perfectly. Besides, you know he loves you, he always has. He'll pay you five hundred, probably. Interested?"

"You know I am, even though I know how much five hundred is in Warren Grant money." He turned his head away from Zena's eyes, and it wasn't for effect. "What do I need to do?"

"Not a thing. I'll call him right now and set it up. You can talk to him yourself. All I want is for you to get the hell out of my life."

• • • •

ZENA COULDN'T HAVE known what she had just set into motion.

Grant gave him the part, not only because he liked him, but because he was still a fan and wanted to see him create art in front of the camera again.

When the cameras rolled, the entire production staff was mesmerized by what they saw. The courage it took to go that far, and that deep, bordered on giving yourself up to an entirely new identity, perhaps permanently. It was a singularly constructed reality to live in, for two minutes and fifty-seven seconds, an open and personal reality that no one had ever seen before.

In fact, the performance was so good that he stole the movie, reducing the one hour and thirty-three minutes of mediocrity into three minutes of acting art that would never be seen again. There was such a depth of conflict and emotion in his performance that it pulled you unconsciously inside the soul of Parnell Gray. You were instantly inside his being, and it carried you on a painful journey of despair and guilt. You didn't want to be there, but it had so much meaning for everyone because, without knowing it, you became Parnell Gray. All of this in just under three minutes.

• • • •

'Cargo' became a sensation. Everyone wanted Cotton Palmer. Every
performance he gave was so good that he eventually got leading roles
in big budget blockbusters.

BUT THEN SOMETHING happened. As soon as he was given
starring roles, those movies flopped. It was soon obvious to everyone
that Palmer was only good for certain character parts, and that was it;
he left the industry again.

He retired to his home in Malibu and lived in his private little
world of drugs and sycophants. They swarmed all over him like the
carcass he'd become.

One day, a well-known film critic stopped by for an interview. He
wanted to do an article on well-known character actors in the history
of film. Most of them had died long ago, but a few remained.

The critic, who shall remain nameless, finished his interview with
one last question. "Why have you abandoned the one person who
helped you get where you are? Everyone in this town knows that she
needs your help right now. Why?"

"I have abandoned no one," said Palmer.

"Zena Powell."

"No one helped me but myself. If she's spreading the lie that she
helped me get where I am today, don't believe a word of it. She's a no
talent whore and always was, and everyone knows that. I'm the one
with the talent, not her."

Then he stood up and escorted the reporter out of his house. "And
if you see her, tell her I said she can go straight to hell."

• • • •

NOT LONG AFTER THAT interview, an article appeared in Film
Daily Magazine. A doctoral student from UCLA's Film School had
written an in-depth treatise on Cotton Palmer's acting in 'Cargo'. In
it, he dismissed the entire movie as garbage except for his analysis of
Cotton Palmers' acting and the depth of his performance, which he

immortalized as the 'most insightful character interpretation ever to grace the silver screen'.

This new notoriety hit the film community like an electric shock. Everyone was watching 'Cargo' again just to see those three minutes. It was studied, copied, and lauded by everyone. In fact, there was even a rumor that Cotton Palmer had gone completely insane because of that role, because he couldn't get out of the part and that he was now in an insane asylum. Of course, it wasn't true, even though every paparazzi intern scoured every asylum within fifty miles of Hollywood.

Then the rumor spread that he had died. They found a few actors in these asylums who had lost their minds for more ordinary reasons, and Zena Powell was one of them. That's when all hell broke loose.

. . . .

IN THE INTERVIEW, SHE once again claimed that she had gotten the role of 'Cargo' for Cotton Palmer. It was her connections that give him his big break. She admitted his performance was fantastic, even monumental, but none of it would have happened if she hadn't stepped in.

As a result, 'Cargo' was re-released across the country. The movie was terrible, again, but the Cotton Palmer groupies, now wearing Parnell Gray costumes, formed fan clubs to watch the movie in groups and wait for his performance. They would repeat his every word as he spoke them, loudly and with the exact emotion it reflected. But they felt alive for two minutes and fifty-seven seconds.

That performance got so big that the studio floated a test rumor that a 'Cargo' sequel was in the works. The reaction was a PR tsunami. A sequel would be worth a billion dollars, guaranteed.

. . . .

BUT IT WAS TOO LATE, according to the best indicator, time.

Billionaire producers like Warren Grant live on their piles of money. Now, at the age of almost ninety-two, he spent the last of his days sitting on his pile and watching his old movies.

It was said that he got bored with his old movies and eventually gave all of his original celluloid copies to the Motion Picture History Museum, except for one.

He wouldn't allow anyone to be with him while he watched the original copy of Cotton Palmer's performance in 'Cargo'. Like millions of others, he watched it over and over again.

When they found him in a Parnell Gray costume, in his projection room, the old celluloid film was still flapping around the projector, with the flickering screen empty.

Of course, the tabloids had a field day when the word got out that he'd left his entire estate of real money to Cotton Palmer, which was the least he could do.

The Migrants: A Photo Album

"**C**ome to think of it, I've never seen her wear makeup either," said Lois, speaking loudly through her right index knuckle.

"Have you ever seen her with a guy?" asked Valerie.

"Nope, or a woman." Lois cackled loud enough that Priscilla could hear her over her shoulder.

• • • •

PRISCILLA WAS A BORN migrant, only she didn't know it. This photo shows her approving forms; notice her fist. This photo shows her being humiliated by co-workers causing her to cover her face. But this next photo shows her quitting her job; notice her expression here; Wistful, not serene. Serenity for lonely women cannot be understood.

The caption on the postcard read 'Michoacán in November'. There was no one to send it to, so she pressed it softly to her lips instead.

Migration Directions: Turn inside out, climb a wall, drink brook water and return it with tears, free climb a dream, jump regrets, repel hate, tempt fate (in case your life depends on it) because there is no way back. Last Step: Debate consequences with any fool you encounter and then count backwards to zero and you're there!

Priscilla arrived, as a Monarch landed like painted air in her hand.

This next photo shows Priscilla and the Monarch exiting the airplane. Engine trouble usually ends on weed-tangled runways. Small towns in Mexico have a way of fooling you with their quaint ways. So do yourself a favor, see small towns as they really are and just be done with them.

She rented a compact car. The little monarch rested on her shoulder, fluttering with anticipation. Priscilla smiled at her co-migrant. This photo captures the exact moment Priscilla named her Beauty.

. . . .

THEY WERE DRIVING ALONG a mountain road as a farm truck came barreling toward them, forcing her to turn right. Her rental bounced off the side of the hill, throwing her out over her heels and into a ditch filled with multi-colored snakes, but the car drove on by itself.

Priscilla pulled herself out of the ditch and climbed back up to the road, broken leg and all. The snakes ignored her, knowing her loneliness would do the job for them. Beauty stayed with her all the way.

As she crawled and limped along the road, dragging her leg behind, she found her rental. It was now a roadside flower stand selling pre-fabricated vigils.

This photo shows Priscilla and Beauty with nothing to lose.

To Monarchs, dead flowers are a repulse. Priscilla closed her eyes as Beauty rested motionless on her wrist.

A gentle breeze carried Beauty up to the fir trees on the horizon. It wasn't long before a kaleidoscope of Monarchs came to Priscilla. They covered her from head to toe. This last photo shows Beauty and her friends, and a very large monarch, on their way home.

Are We a Thing?

T racey wanted to know.

"The long answer is yes," said Fyler.

Tracey looked warily at Fyler. "You mean we are?" she asked. They held hands loosely as they walked through the milling crowds of Times Square. If there was a short answer, he wasn't about to tell her, at least not then.

There was never a doubt that Fyler Stinson loved Tracey Astonish, and vice versa, and they both knew it even though Tracey was insecure about it. It was just that Fyler was always too busy pissing people off. He spent most of his free time pumping iron to protect himself. He had too many years of getting his ass kicked as a kid while learning his craft. There's a lot to learn when you want to be the best disturber you can be, like right now, wearing a MAGA cap and a Black Lives Matter T-shirt at the same time.

This was Times Square in September. The heat usually suffocates in September and it takes its sweet time doing it. It is the most persistent of months, filled with summer's lame duck heat and endless why's. For instance, why end summer and begin the fall if there's no difference?

• • • •

EATME WAS A GIANT WALK-in vending machine on Broadway, the newest incarnation of the old automat. Fyler and Tracey were hungry, but for them, it seemed like the best place to eat. Why? Because it was totally self-contained and so were they because they were from Brooklyn, that's why.

Before they ate their meal, Fyler tipped his hat back and rolled up the sleeve of his T-shirt and then said, "Watch this". She was and wasn't surprised by his new tattoo. It was a cartoon inside a heart of George

Floyd with his knee on Donald Trump's neck; the title was 'I Love You Donald'. When he flexed his arm, the knee bounced up and down.

As they ate, Tracey noticed a police officer eating next to them. He glared at her after he noticed Fyler's tattoo, stood up, wiped his mouth, threw the napkin on his half-eaten sandwich and stopped next to Fyler on his way out.

"I'd be careful if I were you," he said.

"Which you're not, so..."

The cop left and Tracey gave him the look. Fyler flexed for Tracey one more time, before giving her that lovable smirk she'd seen so many times before. She smirked back at him.

· · · ·

THE BLACK LIVES MATTER Shop was right next door to the MAGA Shop in the New American Strip Mall on 43rd St. Business was brisk at both shops. It was time to go back to Brooklyn, but Fyler stopped in front of the MAGA Shop while Tracey had one of her premonitions.

She played with her watch as the MAGA Shop swallowed her man. She couldn't bring herself to look in the window as she could hear yelling and scuffling coming from inside. Fyler came stumbling out, T-shirt ripped, with bruises on his face. He was laughing and smirking his was toward Tracey who had tears in her eyes.

"Quit crying."

She did, sort of.

"Let's go home, Fy."

"Not yet." He said, pointing to the Black Lives Matter Shop and went in.

The first thing that came flying out was the MAGA hat spinning into the gutter, then Fyler, then an angry clerk at the entrance telling him to keep his hatred to himself because he was bad for business. Fyler then sat on the curb and Tracey tried to help him up, but he was too heavy.

That's when the same police officer that gave Fyler the warning in EatMe came along and lifted him up and rested him against a street lamp. At first, the cop didn't say a word and Tracey thanked him for helping.

The cop waited.

"I told you to be careful, son," said the veteran cop.

Fyler stood on his own saying, "No, you didn't. You said if you were me, you'd be careful."

"Some people never learn", was written all over the cop's face as he walked into another day of doubt.

Fyler and Tracey held each other as they walked down the steps of the subway home. Turns out there was no short answer after all.

Microboy Never Loved Christina

"*It ain't what they call you; it's what you answer to.*" — W. C. Fields
We might deny it, but most of us don't like who we are. Sometimes we pretend we're someone else. Maybe we don't know, or maybe we just don't care. Take me, for instance. My name is Carl, but it wasn't when I returned home from work that hot June day in Troy Hills; it was Frank, Frank Stanley.

• • • •

I'M NO GENIUS, BUT it doesn't take one to figure that the power was out. I knew my condo would become like an oven, and it was, so I grabbed a Schlitz Lite from the dead refrigerator and dragged a kitchen chair out to the balcony as I needed some air.

Just as I tried to take in a deep breath, the wind blew dust, and I got a mouthful of sand for my trouble, proving beyond a doubt that keeping your mouth shut is a good idea, not that I've ever put much stock in good ideas.

Oh, and my can of Schlitz Lite. It tasted like shit, so I threw it as far away as I could into the parking lot below.

Boris Yemenski, the short stocky Russian with the pencil mustache who ran the condo complex, ran past my balcony, holding his arms up. I wanted to whine about the power outage, but he ran past too fast, flexing his gun tatts and without breaking stride.

I could see Mrs. Mannering flailing away on her balcony, pushing about seventy in her half-opened kimono that flapped in the wind like a Japanese flag of conquest. She kept pointing at the steel curlers in her hair and waving at Boris to come up and fix her situation. Her dull yellow hair looked like wet straw and her skin was thin and crispy, like fried cellophane. She also usually wore tight dresses.

Before I knew it, she disappeared into her condo, and so did Boris. I didn't see him after that. Management can often be a complex system of tradeoffs and compromises, but I had confidence in Boris.

The storm arrived and my three girlfriends that lived along the river, Justine, Josie and Jewel, were all being shaken like rag dolls by spoiled children. Even trees can become girlfriends when you haven't had a date in a long time. I wondered if Boris was enjoying himself. Then suddenly, something sharp hit my face.

A trickle of blood came out of my right cheek and poured down the front of my shirt. I looked around to find who threw it, but the minute I realized the wind did it, I took it like a man. My exhibition of grace under fire made me feel brave, as I wiped the blood away, keeping my finger on my cheek for modesty that no one saw. I must have looked precious.

For a second, all the lights came on and went off again, but Boris still had time. Then I started having pornographic thoughts about Mrs. Mannering. Her skin became soft and firm, and her breasts became larger and pinker. Her husband worked the night shift at the Walmart on Heath Place.

I could hear Sol Stein's deep booming voice next door. He was blowing word bombs at his son Billie to study hard and make something of himself. Even I knew it was pointless. It was the same speech I'd heard myself, years before, by my own Sol. It was as pointless then as it was now.

My can of Schlitz Lite beer had somehow landed on the roof of Sol's new SUV. That SUV was his pride and joy; the shiny black one with the Tech Package. For a split second, I convinced myself that I threw the brew for Billie. I made myself believe I was Billie's hero and that I could save him.

The roaring wind muffled the rest of Sol's monologue, but not the slamming of the door. I knew Annie Stein was pleading with Billie to stay.

At most, the entire death scene took five seconds. I'd heard gunshots before, so I ducked behind my balcony wall and watched as Billie became an instant memory, unbeknownst to Billie. The passing storm buried Billie in dead leaves and garbage. Hard to know why, but the last thing Billie did was to embrace the left front tire of Sol's pride and joy. Maybe they're right. Maybe we are what we drive, after all.

I decided not to waste my time consoling the Steins. I didn't like them anyway, and I was pretty sure the feeling was mutual. Besides, I could hear the cops' canned consolations, so why bother?

The Steins once told me to leave their son Billie alone and stop giving him bad ideas. I told them how to raise him right and they told me to be the Jew I really was and to stop hiding from the truth. That was the last conversation we ever had, because I thought I'd discovered something new, that there were hypocrites everywhere, which turned out to be a good place to hide for a while.

When I legally changed my name from Stanley Frankowitz to Frank Stanley, I became Frank Stanley, and that was that. A few moments later, the air conditioning came on.

When I woke up the next morning, I felt guilty. Somehow, I killed Billie myself. Somehow, everything changed right then.

I dropped my last moldy bagel into the toaster and hoped for the best, followed by making a lame promise to myself to enjoy my morning despite the slide-show of death that kept shuffling and reshuffling itself in my head. It wouldn't quit, even when I went back to the balcony to see if it had all been a bad dream. But there was Sol, in the parking lot, cleaning the Schlitz off the roof of his SUV. He was standing on the chalk outline of Billie's head.

I went back inside and Googled for myself anything to stop the slideshow. And then that loop started all over again.

It took a while, but I finally found myself. I was number 68 of 12,761, on page four. Then I read my mother's fake maiden name, and the loop stopped.

• • • •

LIKE MOST HOME SECURITY companies, 'Tracers' was a scam. The day I was hired by 'Tracers' as a programmer, I had 'opted out' of sharing any of my personal information. To be on the safe side, I planted a marker in my data in case they didn't comply with their promise of confidentiality. Sometimes, it's better to be stupid than naïve.

Peter Browning, CEO of Tracers, had an Open-Door Policy which went like this, "My door is always open but I'm not, so come on in." What angered Pete wasn't that I walked in unannounced or that I angrily threw a printout of my Google ID on his desk, but it was that I replaced his face on the twenty screens in his office with my Personnel Profile.

"What's that?" asked the CEO.

"It's me... Pete."

"So?"

"I opted out of sharing my personal data."

Pete quickly speed-dialed Personnel. "Cut Frank Stanley's last check and have it ready for him in five minutes. He's on his way out."

As he ended that call, he looked up at me and smiled. The streaks of sunlight that pierced through his windows made broken diamonds across his face and gray streaked hair. "You know what your problem is, Frank?" I refused to answer. He waited and waited and waited some more.

"Values Frank, you've got values." His white teeth glistened in the sunlight as he smiled at me and extended his hand from behind his desk. I smiled back and walked out.

Charlie and Mike met me at Payroll and handed me a cardboard box with my stuff. They were the two Security Guards who escorted me out and made me believe that they didn't know me. I tried to think like they must have been in thought at that moment, but I couldn't.

I was free now, except that damn loop came back!

• • • •

THERE WERE STILL A couple of weeks left before the new school year would start.

Ten years had changed nothing. New York City smelled the same. I didn't get why the hope I was feeling felt like anger. But then I got it right away when I passed a head-phoned man walking up the stairs at the Union Square Station. For no apparent reason, just the sight of me must have pissed him off as he told me to go fuck myself. I thanked him for his feedback and continued down the stairs.

As I waited for the train to take me back to Brooklyn, I tried to guess what the 'L' in L Train stood for. 'Loser' became my only choice when I realized that journeys back are never multiple choice.

The hissing of the closing doors sounded final. I looked up at an ad above the doors and it showed an older man and maybe his granddaughter, walking by themselves on a snow-white beach. The caption read: "Don't let your retirement stop you from enjoying your life." The sky above us was a blue I'd never seen before and a palm tree bent away from the water.

It was now me and my backpack, riding an empty subway car, and holding on as the train picked up too much speed and started rocking like a laundromat washing machine.

The old man from the ad was walking towards me, but he kept looking over his shoulder at the young girl, wobbling her way towards him in the careening train. She held her arms out, aiming herself at him.

The screeching train jolted to a stop, and the doors flew open. When I looked around, the two of them were gone.

The sign at the Saratoga Avenue Station was decorated with that colorful, confident graffiti —the kind they now call art even though it isn't. I could see from the platform that the old neighborhood was still filthy. The flying white horse was now full of bullet holes, but it was still flying above the gas station, now abandoned.

The heavy thumping beat coming from Camacho's Latin Music Store gave everything a pulse and the screaming sirens crying wolf, gave it a voice.

Everything I owned was in my backpack. The weight of it pushed me down the elevated subway station stairs faster than I wanted to go. Soon after, three Puerto Rican bullies surrounded me at the bottom of the stairs. One of them squeezed my backpack like a mango. As a chorus, they asked me if I was Jewish. I told them no, and they laughed and asked me for money. I thanked them for their request, but asked them if they would like to die because I killed for dope. They flicked their cigarette butts at me and walked away.

As I walked, the smell of plantain chips frying in rancid oil hit me hard. Then the fresh stench of rotting garbage and backed up sewers took over. I witnessed what happens when you take recycling too seriously, as the scavengers ate the garbage and the drunks drank the sewage.

I turned the corner and there it was, 945 Dumont Ave, which used to be 945 MLK Boulevard, which used to be 945 Ithaca Ave.

A busybody woman in curlers, no comparison to Mrs. Mannering, was yelling at the top of her lungs out of a 4th floor window at maybe her son to stop talking to hoodlums and go to work already before they'd fire him. She looked at me to see if I agreed. My pretended neutrality was weak and no match for her eyes and the smile on her face, which thanked me for agreeing with her.

Right away, I remembered it took little to live there, or die there but I didn't have a coin to flip to see which one was mine. The buzzer that lets you in was on a permanent buzz, so all you had to do was push, which I did. I should have known better.

I couldn't tell where he was from, but after demonstrating some sign language like opening a door with a key, the dirty T-shirt landlord gave me the key to the dump I was about to call home. The sound of my footsteps echoed off the stone walls like bad acid trip elevator music.

The one lyric to the song was on the wall, 'Micro Boy loves Christina 4eVer'.

Apartment 202 caught me by surprise. I'd forgotten about Alex. He used to live there with his mother. He moved back to Poland after she killed herself. Not that I was an expert on the subject, but since then, I've learned that people die all the time.

202's brown metal door was stuck shut so I kept hitting it with my shoulder.

A young black kid came running up the stairs and he gave me a smirk of approval. I smirked back and told him to go fuck himself. Then he grabbed his crotch at me and glided up the stairs, four steps at a time. I couldn't figure out why his footsteps were silent.

• • • •

PRINCIPAL MARCIA KAPLAN hadn't aged gracefully, but her arrogance must have discovered the fountain of youth.

"Had I known it was you, Stanley, I wouldn't have hired you. But since it's too late to do anything about it right now, I'll have to live with my decision, for now."

"Marcia, if I can call you Marcia, I can teach these kids. I know I can."

"No."

"No, what?"

"No, you can't call me Marcia. You can call me Principal Kaplan. Familiarity breeds contempt, and so on."

The pencil she was stabbing the air with broke as she jabbed her desk with it. Her arrogance had morphed into road rage, which was difficult to do when you are sitting behind a desk. But she pumped the brakes a little.

"Tell me, why did you change your name, Stanley?"

"Well, your name isn't Principal Kaplan, now is it, Marcia? Why should I call you something you're not, Marcia?"

That statement goosed her as she stood up and rearranged her black outfit, curling her finger at me. She hadn't changed and the Intermediate School 242 that used to be Junior High School 242, hadn't changed either. And although I thought I knew the answer already, I was about to find out if the students had changed.

She fast-walked me up to my classroom, where the students had already made themselves comfortable. As the door opened in front of her, she poked her head in.

"Class, I want to introduce Mr. Stanley. He's your new homeroom teacher. Please make him feel welcome."

Marcia was still pretty strong as she shoved me in from behind. A loud fart came from the back of the classroom and many of the students laughed, but a few didn't.

"Yep, smells like Stanley," said a female voice from the back.

Kaplan slammed the door.

They all had smart phones which they held like crucifixes.

"If you're going to throw stuff at me when I turn around, do me a favor and wait a second so I can take my selfie with you first."

Nothing came next. I sat on my chair with my legs up on the desk, ignoring them while they played video games with each other. When it was time for them to go to their next class, I still ignored them. As they walked out, a few of them tried to look at what I was doing on my phone.

On my second day, I found my way into their Instagram, Twitter, and Facebook accounts. For a while, my meme was anonymous. Then they got it and they were good with it. In fact, a few of them thought it was pretty funny and then a few more wanted to know how I did it. These were the naturally curious ones. Maria Gomez was one of them. She was bright, inquisitive, positive, and everyone's friend. I figured out quickly that gaining her trust was critical. She quietly spread the word that they needed to give me a chance to prove myself, and it worked.

Even the diehards gave in, but it took a full two months, which put them behind in the school curriculum.

I made sure I told them as often as I could that I would never betray their trust, no matter what, but I had to prove it.

Then we flipped roles. They taught me their Family Rules. Rule #1 - Every member of the family had to be available to the others 24/7 — not the fake 24/7, the real 24/7. So, I made myself available to all of them whenever they needed me.

Curriculums — not the reasons they exist — have to be followed. So I worked the curriculum into our social media account. At first, they snapped to it but ignored it. But when I turned it into a video game called "Beat the System", their test scores zoomed up to the top of all the other classes in the school. They actually beat the system or curriculum or whatever you want to call the thing that should keep them down. People took notice, but Marcia thought I had taught them how to cloak their cheating.

Unfortunately for Marcia, the students actually started learning. Unfortunately for me, success breeds contempt.

Dejuan Howard earned his living as a P.E. teacher, but earned his favor by snitching. He was the self-appointed hall monitor that spent all his free time, including lunch breaks, roaming the hallways and looking for opportunities.

The School Policy of, "No open windows for the safety of our students", could not under any circumstances, be broken. What was supposed to be breathable air in our classroom wasn't. Therefore, an Einstein moment happened. I opened the windows.

"In case any of you are planning on jumping out of these windows, please don't."

The two-cough warning from Ersie Jefferson made it clear that the snitch was looking. Everyone ignored the snitch but knew exactly what was coming. I saw him when I was in the middle of a Social Studies lesson on the Declaration of Independence. In less than two minutes, Marcia, in red, appeared at the door, doing her finger curl.

"And don't forget students, at the same time that George Washington, the Father of our country, declared that all men were created equal, he was wearing dentures made from the teeth of his own slaves."

"Can I see you for a second, Mr. Stanley?"

"Certainly Marcia, excuse me for one second class."

"Mr. Howard, please take over while I speak to Mr. Stanley in my office."

The smirking snitch glowed.

At that point in the school year, my six-day suspension was the end of my career. So, I walked home as the texts poured in. The one that made me feel the best was the one from Maria. It was uplifting, kind and thanked me for standing up for all the Family members and that they were all behind me. I thanked her for her kindness.

I felt funny walking home. The heat wave in the city smothered everything. There was one window in my apartment that could be opened, which led out to the fire escape. Unfortunately, there was no fire and there was no escape, so I waited for more words, but none came.

Two hours later, a text came from Ersie. It said that Maria had been killed by a speeding taxi as she crossed Saratoga Ave. "She was texting you, Mr. Stanley, and not paying attention to the traffic. She was killed just before sending you the text."

I texted the Family that I was on my way to Maria's home. I knew that no matter what I would tell her parents, it couldn't replace Maria. The death of a child is deafening and unfair. The tears of her friends couldn't even console Sixto and Soledad, Maria's parents. Everyone told me it wasn't my fault, but the look in Sixto's eyes felt like daggers.

Marcia fired me into her office. None of her words made their way into my brain except 'you caused this' and 'irresponsible'. Those words I knew.

As I passed the family in the hallway, I turned off my phone as I couldn't look at them.

• • • •

I DIDN'T LIKE IT MUCH, sitting on a park bench, and getting rained on, off and on.

"You should listen to him, you know. He's got something important to tell you," said an old man in a Mets cap who had stopped in front of me. He pointed his umbrella at a nearby tree.

"That bird, the little red one up there in the tree. His name is Silhouette."

Then he sat down next to me and introduced his Chihuahua. "His name is Cupcake; in case you're interested."

"I'm not."

Looking up at the sky didn't work. The dog gave me a low growl, which was amusing since he had no teeth. I tried the sky strategy again.

"I bought the ashes of Somerset Maugham years ago at a Flea Market on Pitkin Avenue, tripped out in India and sold digital Christmas lights to Tibetan Monks in the Himalayas. To this day, mind you, to this day I do not know how I got back home," he said, shrugging off his own words. Then the dog growled at me again.

"What's his problem?"

"Nothing. It's just that you remind him of someone. He's seen a photograph of this person for his whole life, so he thinks he knows him." He paused for a second and cupped his hand over his mouth and whispered to me like we'd known each other forever. "But he doesn't really know him. But I have to agree, there is a resemblance." He gently patted the dog's head and said, "He's ok baby, he's ok."

He continued on saying, "I spread the ashes on the heating rocks of a Brighton Beach shvitz and inhaled as much of it as I could. But in case that wouldn't work, I kept some in a shot glass in my kitchen cabinet as a backup. I thought that if I put it in a glass of warm tea, one day, and drank it, I could channel Maugham, when I finally got around to writing my novel, which I never did, by the way."

"Why?"

"Why? Because after I drank that glass of tea, I debated with myself for twenty-three years about whether drinking his ashes was the same thing as cannibalism. Couldn't figure it out, so, well, here I am, still debating... But if I do, I've got the title for it. It will be called 'Sanity as a Second Language. The User Manual.'" He nodded slightly, as if he agreed with his own indecision.

I had a feeling he wouldn't stop.

"My story cannot be stopped. It's like this rain." And right on cue, the rain started again, so he opened his umbrella over both of us. "It feeds my flow, which is an out-of-control river. It goes on forever, whatever forever is." He caught his breath. "You would think that by now I would have figured it all out, being the broken-down piece of shit that I am. It's unfortunate, though. There are too many things to figure out when you get old."

I thought I'd finally reached my limit, so I stood up to leave. But the old man gently pulled me back and handed me what looked like a plain white business card. It read, "Murray the Bitch, F.B.A."

"What's an F.B.A.?"

"Freelance Bullshit Artist. I'm a salesman. I create it and sell it. For instance, for you, here's what I would tell you. You can't feast on life if your dessert is regret. And I'm sure you're thinking to yourself, that's bullshit, which it is, but maybe not. And that's my point; I can't stop lying. So, no matter what I tell you, even if I tell you it's a lie, you'll still want more."

"Listen, I lie to myself all the time. I don't need any help from you."

"Actually, you do," insisted Murray. "You'll see. Oh, and in case you want to know, I'm also on the web. Actually, I used to have my own YouTube Channel until they deleted it, which is too bad really. No matter though, because now I live inside the Dark Web under the alias 'Jack Webb in Drag', not dragnet. All Jack wanted were facts. Not me. Why? Because facts are bullshit. All I want are lies that sell the hell with facts. So, if you would like me to provide regular lies, it will cost you a flat $15/Month, which is my entry level Plan called UB, Unlimited Bullshit. Want another free sample?"

"No."

"Ok, remember that everything I'm going to tell you is bullshit. So, here you are, sitting on this bench and I decide to sit down next to you, right?"

"Yeah, so?"

"Then I told you about my journey through my Hindu Hell and my cannibalistic tendencies as a neophyte writer, right?"

I couldn't respond because I became paralyzed by my boredom.

"Ok, listen carefully because this is the crux. Are you sure you're listening?"

"Yes."

"Ok. Cancer is nothing more than a manifestation of Schopenhauer's Will. That's right. It's the force that's everywhere, all the time. Everyone gets some of it, but some people, for whatever reason, get an excess amount because it has a mind of its own. For example, no one is immune from insanity, which emerges like thunder from within, and when it arrives, it can't be stopped. So, what happens when insanity fights cancer? Simple, you have Communism in a no-revolution takeover. Everything works for the good of the people. So, if you die, so be it."

"So what?"

Murray answered, "Exactly. Because Communistic entrepreneurs like myself control their own destinies, for the good of the people, of course. The sample I just gave you was a teaser. There's more, in fact there's always more. And, if you doubt me, remember this: once you become a subscriber, it will be, I promise you, all about you! So, just keep that in mind. You will be your own addiction, and you'll never be able to get enough of yourself, which is covered by the fee. You will become the dope of you."

· · · ·

ETERNITY CAN COME IN many forms. Mine came in a two-week package of boredom and self- pity, not to mention isolation. I talked to no one, including the old man and his Chihuahua named Cupcake, who was walking by my favorite bench in Betsy Head Park. No telling what would come out of his mouth.

"Hey. Hey you, Murray, I'm ready to be a member."

He gently stopped. "If you are, remember that everything I'm going to tell you is bullshit." He held up one finger and added, "But, included with your UB, are 'free' nuggets of what is known as The Truth. However, there's a kicker. The amount of the Truth will change from time to time."

I couldn't tell if Cupcake was nodding in approval or just breathing hard, but Murray wanted to talk about Add-Ons.

"The percentage of Truth you get depends on the level you're buying. Your basic UB, Unlimited Bullshit, comes with a standard plus or minus ten percent truth. But you can buy up to one hundred percent Truth if you choose, but even I have to admit, it's a little pricey. And the truth is never revealed. And, if you recall, even Truth is bullshit."

"I recall."

"Ok, are you ready?"

"I am."

So I took out my last ten and five dollars and handed them to Murray. He wouldn't take it and smiled with a quiet, "Don't worry about that now." It took him a while to sit down on the bench and put Cupcake on his lap.

"Ok, there was a time when I became my own Rorschach Test. I lived in a world of robot memes. No matter where I went, they surrounded me. When I left the Himalayas, I found myself in Plato's Cave. Shadows of Reality are Greek for bullshit. By the way, it's actually in Turkey, not Greece — the cave, I mean. Did you know Turkey exists in dual but separate parallel dimensions? One exists in the pre-dawn apocalypse and the other in a totalitarian agnostically religious state of semi-democracy. Is it Troy or Gobekli Tepe? Who knows, but I saw tracers from my inner bitch directing me away from the real me, which was dead or didn't exist. Take your pick. Also, did you know these things die as soon as you think about them? That fast," he said, snapping his fingers in my face.

"Ok Murray, who the fuck are you?"

"Who am I? Good question. I'll tell you who I am. I'm the Fourth Stooge. That's who I am. It was Moe who christened me Bitchy. Don't let anyone tell you that Schlep was the Fourth. I met Moe at a Think Tank in Santa Barbara, where we were both submerged in a viscous liquid of Hollywood Showbiz urine and raw sewage from San Quentin. Believe it or not, you can actually think of that shit, but don't ask me how. Anyway, we were finally flushed out of there and we found ourselves in the Cemetery State known as Popularity, as defined by the Wikipedia Encyclopedia of Illiterate Excuses. So what I learned from that experience is this; I should have taken Moe's slaps, not as hate from an asshole, but as Love from a corpse. So, I left that cemetery as a mist in the twilight and started out my career as a Freelance Bullshit Artist. Does that answer your question?"

After I answered "Yes", I walked home shaking my head like an old Chihuahua.

. . . .

HE HAD AN HONEST WAY of dealing with questions that weren't questions. For instance, I asked him this question, since he said it would be all about me;

"What's worse, knowing the Truth or dealing with it?"

"The Cult of The Ignorant is populated by the Goat People of Stupidia. I learned this in the Sudan, where a local tribal chieftain bought my ass on the black market, which is not restricted to blackness. He believed I was a white shaman in a reverse dream sequence of never-ending fantasies fueled by drugs, intellectual pomposity and linguistic slights-of-hand. The Truth, which for you is now Thirty Percent, is that as a slave to him, I learned the true value of freedom—which ain't much, despite what you've probably been told."

"What I've already learned is that freedom has no value, and neither does truth. They just are."

"Exactly, because Freedom is Fear. The only Freedom you will ever know is and can only be Experience," texted Murray.

"I'm pretty sure I know Fear."

"No, you don't."

"Oh yes, I do."

"I was in denial once myself, when I lived with a cult that believed in vegetarianism as a way of life. They sacrificed their children to their Great God, Algo Rithma, who predicted with great accuracy when and where each child would die at the hands of their parents. So, their mantra, which was "Eat a Carrot, Kill a Kid", took hold of me for ten years until I actually realized that they had it all wrong, backwards in fact. It actually was, and this ended my denial, which is where I am right now, "Eat a kid, Kill a Tree". My Maugham Smoothie was my validation."

"And you denied it was the right thing to do?"

"No, I was in denial that it was part of Schopenhauer's Will and that I had absolutely no say, per se, in denying it. See?"

"Not really."

"Well, take my latest self-hack, for example. I'm going to build a giant phallic symbol out of Legos and start a new Fund Me campaign for Phallic Freedom of Thought. And what you might ask me is, what is Phallic Freedom of Thought? It is the promotion of an intellectual environment wherein you will think and live phallically without religious, governmental or social recrimination of any kind."

"Sounds pretty useless."

"Well, we all do it anyway. Why not do it without fear or worry?"

"I thought you said Freedom is Fear."

"Being free isn't always desirable. We're all hooked on Will as our permanent addiction anyway, so taking methadone for our addictions with a little fake freedom is ok. My Fund Me campaign is just a minor intervention, just a minor diversion, really. And, of course, a few extra bucks never hurt."

· · · ·

SOMETIMES, THE SOUND of laughter can either make you sick or make you wonder why you didn't get it.

I was sitting on my rusty fire escape when I heard laughter from the fire escape above.

It was Murray and Cupcake. The old man was laughing and his dog was lip-syncing. They were like an old married couple finishing each other's thoughts and mouthing each other's words. No wonder they were laughing.

"That you Murray?" He kept laughing.

"We were just discussing how easy it is these days to make a buck. A man has to earn a living, you know. No getting around it. Look at me, I sold my T.V., bought a laptop, got a smart phone, changed my look, got subscribers and now look at me. I'm living off the land."

"There's no land in Brownsville."

"Oh yes, there is," he answered, raising his left eyebrow. "It's the land of where you really live, of course, if you choose to live there.

You can GPS your ass or live in the big Strip Joint in the Sky getting lap dances from the Grim Reaper, that's where. Ever see a ninety-three-year-old Brooklyn Jew in skinny jeans?"

"Inspect." He stood up and showed me his trendy jeans, electric orange sneakers and tight-fitting T-shirt that had something written on the front in large black letters. "See?"

"What's it say?"

He pointed to the words. "It says, 'Nothing but Net Bitch.'" Then he slowly crawled back through his window and into his apartment. I did not know that he lived right above me in 302, the apartment I grew up in.

He poked his head back out of his window and said, "It was a gift from my so-called friends."

• • • •

I FOUND OUT SOON ENOUGH that his 'so-called friends' were mostly the 369.

Who they were mattered little to them or anyone else that lived in the building. Most of them hung out in front of Murray's place, and a few in front of the building. As far as I was concerned, I had enough stuff to worry about, so I never gave them much thought.

They were mostly young men and a few girls, and if reputations mattered, they were supposed to be ruthless. They had a lot of money from whatever they did. Was killing included in whatever? Probably.

At first, I couldn't figure out why they tolerated me. All I knew was that their friendly nods felt good. Maybe it was Murray or maybe it was the Family, but one thing I soon realized was that it wasn't dumb luck.

By July 4th, my independence and freedom ran out. I ran out of money and food and I couldn't pay my rent.

Then things started appearing at my door, like food in cardboard boxes, and a loose twenty, usually tucked in there somewhere, or sometimes folded into a paper airplane, in case I needed some entertainment.

· · · ·

I COULDN'T ACCEPT THE gifts, so I left them with a note thanking them for their kindness.

Instead, I walked to the Super 3 and ambled around like the unprofessional shoplifter I was. The owner wasn't fooled for a second and slammed me up against the chicharron rack. The roll and lunch meat fell out from under my shirt.

"Call the cops Frankie. I'm sick of these assholes stealing everything I've got. I'm sick of it."

Frankie, the security guard at the Super 3, was an off-duty moonlighting cop that had worked in the neighborhood for a long time. He pulled the owner aside and whispered in his ear.

The owner picked up the roll and meat and shoved it in my chest. Then he told me to get the fuck out and don't come back, ever again. I didn't say a word, and I didn't apologize. Hunger equalizes everything, including humiliation. I'd tasted nothing that good before or since.

I went to Murray's for dessert.

"I had a friend once," said Murray as his eyes teared up. "His name was Carl. We drank schnapps together. We organized unions and even joined the Merchant Marine together. But he died first and I've been waiting for his phone call ever since." He paused for a minute. "You may be Carl and I can't take the chance that you aren't, so allow me to put a little schnapps in your tea and give you a welcome home hug."

He poured some whiskey in my tea and we spent the rest of the afternoon talking about the differences between law and justice and about the last man to actually think one completely clear thought, Socrates, who by the way, according to Murray, wasn't as smart as people thought he was. But, his one clear thought, "nothing to be preferred before justice" was pure genius, but the rest of his so-called philosophy wasn't much.

"When you live inside the Dark Web," said Murray, "you're homeless. This is a fact that can't be denied and everyone who lives there, well, they're all homeless. It's actually a requirement for living there. It only asks your Social Security Number. Then you get the Code of Life."

• • • •

WHENEVER I COULDN'T sleep or whenever I felt the sorriest for myself, I somehow found myself in Murray's apartment. As usual, his door was wide open and there were a few 369's hanging out. One of them, who I found out later was Micro Boy, was sitting next to Murray on his old worn-out brown corduroy sofa. They were having a Rap Chat, tapping out the beat on the sofa. It went something like this:

Murray - "Tell me why you die.

Tell me why you die."

Young Man - "The Truth Bitch

The Truth Bitch

The Truth Bitch."

Murray - "All I do is lie about the Truth

The Truth ain't shit.

This shit's gotta go.

This shit has got to go."

Young Man - "Tell me bitch, I ain't shit.

I ain't shit and I'm baffling.

I love her and I'm baffling.

Baffling kills babies.

Baffling lives till you die."

That conversation went on for another thirty minutes. They could see me standing there, listening, but it didn't matter. The young man got up, kissed Murray on the top of his head, and said. "I feel you bitch, I feel you."

Murray answered. "Ok, but don't fuck with me. You feel me now?"

The young man didn't answer right away, but after he thought about it, he smiled and said, "Yeah, I feel you." As the young man left, Murray pulled him back, gave him a hug, slapped him on his ass and sent him on his way.

Everyone, except for one guard, left, because they could see that the old man was tired. I hung out with him for a while. Murray sat back down and closed his eyes; he slept deep and free. I monitored him for a while and thought about how much I loved teaching children, like he did.

When Murray finally woke up, he said, "I'm going to call you Carl from now on and all of my so-called friends will also call you Carl. Why? Because Carl would have liked that." He fell asleep again, and I left, leaving the front door open, as always.

• • • •

AUGUST IS TECHNICALLY not a month, and here's why.

It was August 11th, and Murray's door was closed. That's why. I knocked on it loud enough to wake the dead, which, in this case, turned out to be Bertha Sexton, Murray's next-door neighbor.

"If you're looking for Murray, don't waste your time. He's in jail. The old fool."

"Thank you, Bertha. I found Cupcake barking in front of my door."

"That dog's as stupid as that old fool, maybe stupider."

The Legion Street jail was in the back of the Police Station. I talked my way in to see Murray, who looked happy to see me. He grinned out a big smile and flashed gold braces that covered his dentures. Some kind of code was printed on them.

He looked like he needed a straight man, so I volunteered.

I pointed to his mouth and said, "What the hell is that?"

"It's The Code of Life, which is now my message to the world. As soon as you see it, you immediately get it. But if you don't, well, then you're not one of my so-called friends."

He whispered it in my ear. "Now you know, Carl."

The cops released him to me, pending further investigation. There had been a sting operation on The 369 and Murray got caught in the net. None of The 369 said they knew him and that he just was walking by.

As we left the station, there were reporters waiting outside. Murray flashed The Code of Life smile and pointed to his mouth with a peace sign. We got on the bus that took us home and when we got off the bus, he paused for a moment and gently put his finger on my chest. "Don't ever believe that FDR was a Fellow Traveler. He force-fed America gold-plated gag-proof geese that were cooked in the heat of battle, not the one from WWII, but the real one called Economic Instability, which entailed false work for fake money to cure a sickness caused by greedy capitalists who jumped out of windows and landed on pillows filled with counterfeit fortunes."

We walked home slowly from the bus stop. "Come have lunch with me and bring You-Know-Who. I miss him."

I retrieved You-Know-Who, Cupcake's new alias, and returned him to the old man and when I did, the old man's eyes smiled. We ate soft-boiled eggs, Gruyère cheese triangles, the kind that came covered in foil, pumpernickel bread and butter and, of course, hot tea. It was good, but my hunger returned. I left Murray's door open when he fell asleep, and I didn't want to look back.

• • • •

• • • •

WITH THE NEW SCHOOL year approaching, tweets poured in from the Family, wanting me to teach again. I kept finding more stray twenties from someone under my door. I needed answers.

Murray was sitting on his corduroy sofa in his underwear and Mets cap. Another faded copy of The Daily Worker was in his hands as he read again.

As he read it, he laughed out loud and then looked up at me and said, "The symphony of the blind is the silence of the deaf. He's gone now, but he was a very smart man."

He stopped his monologue and returned to his reading. I read the back page while he read his memories. It was a full-page ad for a Trade Union Meeting of Furriers in the Garment District. Whoever went to that meeting was probably dead by now.

Murray looked up at the ceiling. "It's easy to Stalinize a Rockefeller bum. All you have to do is throw him a dime and promise him happiness and security." Then he closed his eyes. "In 1938, Stalin and Gandhi had a bromance, a little-known fact. It developed rapidly from there, and they had an illegitimate son named Murray. Want some tea?"

"Yes."

"I learned how to brew tea in Cambodia when I was part of a kibbutz in Phnom Penh. I was hired as a Cultural Envoy for the Cambodian Government, by Slowmo, believe it or not, who had been contracted by the Cambodian Government to clarify Confucianism for the people, the Cambodian people, that is. The Chinese weren't confused, because they invented it, which I'm still not totally convinced of. Anyway, I was supposed to start the first Cambodian Kibbutz. And I'll tell you this: Kibbutz's not in Israel are hard enough to establish, but in Cambodia, well, you can just imagine. Then, for whatever reason, we thought we could homestead in Angkor Wat, which had been designated as a Dead Zone. Well, we succeeded for a while and besides learning how to brew tea, we also learned how to cry in tongues. I eventually left Cambodia when a comic, who shall remain nameless, did USO Shows for all Jews left behind in Concentration Camps that had been converted into Kibbutz's by the Russians. But then, as fate would have it, his bird became paralyzed and his mind froze when he lost his shtick, more commonly known as the ability to make people laugh. And when he started his own Cable Show, Demolition Derby for Washed-Up Catskillians, the same thing happened to me. I didn't have any shtick to lose, but I used to have what is known as sanity. I lost my sanity to a girl named Sheila who twisted my arm to become a Catholic. She lived somewhere in Indiana. When I finally told her no because I was a Hindi of the lowest caste, sweeping up cow shit and calling it my pleasure, she cried like a baby and kicked my ass out into the street — a full twenty feet to the curb, mind you. I call it Demolition Derby, Murray style."

He took in a breath but kept staring at me, like he suddenly recognized me. I went along with my new identity and slept well that night. In the morning, when I woke up, I found another twenty under my door with a note attached to it. It read:

"Carl,
Thought you could use this.
My so-called friends are working
on your situation. I anticipate
good results.
Murray
P.S. Great to have you back"

· · · ·

I SAW LITTLE MURRAY after that. Occasionally, I would pass by his door to see how he was doing and would usually see him rapping with different kids, texting on his phone or reading his Daily Workers. This time, looked frail and sadder as Cupcake wasn't around anymore.

· · · ·

THE SUMMER WENT BY hot and slow. I got by somehow with help from friends and 'so-called' friends. Two weeks before the school year was supposed to start, a grass-roots campaign had me reinstated to my old teaching position. There were student protests in front of the school and in front of Kaplan's home.

Maybe Kaplan and the Board had had enough. They offered to reinstate me if I would relent in my use of social media to teach. I told them 'no' and walked out of her office. The students somehow knew I declined her offer and cheered me as I left. Over the next few days, the protests grew.

I kept to myself as much as possible as the new school year approached. Two days before the school year began, the heat forced me out on my fire escape again. There were indistinct murmurs coming from Murray's place, so I went upstairs and saw a small group of his so-called friends who had gathered around him. When I entered, the crowd put their arms around me and, as I looked at Murray, I knew he was dead.

• • • •

IF YOU'RE FREE, YOU should be afraid, according to Murray. I felt both free and afraid. That's why I legally changed my name again. I was now Carl, officially. I bitched about everything to everyone.

Maybe, just maybe, I became a consultant to the New York City Board of Education on their New Ventures in Education Through Social Media. Or maybe I became a liaison to the Dark Web. Or maybe we're all Thirty Percent Subscribers. But, as long as we can make our own decisions, we can decide for ourselves who we are and who we want to be. That's Freedom, Murray Style.

The Coat on the Chair

Flight 768 from Toronto had been delayed by bad weather. Carlton Waters looked around the waiting area. It had been a long trip for the CEO of Denver Investment Associates, and he was disappointed when he didn't see his wife and son. It was 2 a.m.

The lanky 63-year-old executive took his usual long strides to the baggage claim area. Suitcases, old tied-up boxes, and worn-out guitar cases slid out clumsily from the black hole. He thought his suitcase would come out first because, well after all, he was Carlton Waters, but they came out last.

The freezing Denver air felt good and was inhaled even better. Waters was a powerful man, easily tossing his bag into the trunk of his self-driving Jag. He felt stupid telling it to take him home because he knew he could drive home faster on his own, but in keeping with his 'stay young' workarounds, he let the car take over.

He and Jen loved each other despite what most people thought. Why would a young, attractive woman like Jen, marry an old asshole like himself? Was Brian his grandson? Listen, grandsons matter little. Besides, Brian was the son he'd always wanted and became the best part of his life.

The road out of Denver International Airport was coated in black ice, causing his Jag to move into all-wheel drive. Carlton knew it would make the trip longer than it had to be. A bad car wreck on the other side of the freeway caused the traffic to almost stop. Waters felt the intense heat coming off the wreck when he opened his window. He pissed himself off when he did the same thing all the other idiots do when they see carnage like that.

"Bob," the name he gave his car even though he thought naming devices with human names was stupid, "Call Jen." The call wouldn't go through. She always picked up, no matter the time, because they had an agreement.

• • • •

JEN'S CAR WASN'T IN the garage as Bob drove in, turned on the lights and told C.W. that they had arrived at their destination, like he didn't know. Everything puzzled Waters; a few of Brian's toys were scattered in the living room, a few dirty dishes were left in the sink, and the T.V. in the bedroom had been left on. Putting the pieces together, he came up with nothing, except that maybe they had to leave in a hurry. Maybe Brian got sick, and she had to take him to a doctor. Maybe her sister got sick, and she had to go take care of her, which didn't make complete sense because Carole was married to Porter, a cardiologist. So, he called Carole.

"She told me she was going with Brian to the airport to surprise you," responded Carole.

"She wasn't there, and she's not here. Gotta go Carole, think I heard something. I'll call you back. Maybe it's Jen."

• • • •

THE SENIOR POLICE OFFICER munched loudly on pork skins as his junior partner drove to Silver Lode Drive.

"If there's no one home, everyone's probably dead. If there's someone home, they have no clue about what happened and I'm the one who has to tell them. Why is it always me?" asked Officer Daniel Majeski, causing his faint smile to disappear.

"I...," was all that the younger Lonnie Jackson could say before his partner jumped in.

"I'll tell you why. Because Captain Mallory hates my guts and always puts me on Graveyard, that's why. Ever since I gave his senile father a speeding ticket, which he deserved, he's had it in for me. It's revenge, plain and simple," said Majeski as he pointed to the large house that belonged to C.W. "There, there's the house. Pull over."

"OK..."

Majeski got out of the patrol car. "No, you stay here." The lights were on in the house. He finished his skins, tossed the empty bag on the lawn like he was making a three-point shot, and rang the doorbell. In less than a second, he wiped his greasy hands on the front door instead of his uniform and rang the doorbell.

The look on C.W.'s face gave Majeski a thrill.

"Good evening, sir. Are you the owner of a Black Cadillac Escalade, license SPT 389?"

"Yes."

"There's been an accident."

"What do you mean, accident?"

"A traffic accident, for Pete's sake," said Majeski as he tried but couldn't figure out how to turn off his body cam. "And what is your name, sir?"

"Carlton Waters. What kind of traffic accident?"

"Who is Jennifer Waters?"

"My wife."

"It rear-ended a tanker truck on the road to the airport and was destroyed in the fire. Nothing left but the license plate, which was how we knew to come here."

Carlton Waters stared at Police Officer.

"Sorry for your loss, Mr. Waters. Here's my card," said Majeski. He picked up the empty bag of pork skins as he left and put it in the mailbox.

"How did it go?" asked Jackson.

"Fine, I guess. The old guy took it well."

"Bad news like that..."

"Oh, don't you worry about him. From the looks of his house, he's got plenty. He'll find himself another wife real fast. Believe me, money talks to women. He won't care after a while. Let's get out of here. Places like this make me sick."

• • • •

THE EARLY MORNING AIR that Monday in January, had gotten even colder and was now almost too cold to breathe as Bob roamed downtown Denver. C.W. couldn't hear his new playlist featuring, "You have reached your final destination", "recalculating", and "making a legal U-Turn", as it kept shuffling and re-shuffling. Autonomous Bob was not a mind reader.

How he finally arrived at his destination fell somewhere between Artificial Intelligence and dumb luck, not that it mattered much because C.W. had no clue where he was, what he was doing there, or why it even mattered. Bob edged in like he knew what he was doing. 'CEO' was printed on the parking space's sign. The sign on the mirrored glass building read 'Denver Investment Associates'. The rising sun's reflection off the giant glass monolith was too brilliant to take, but not for Carlton Waters.

Before he entered the building, he stopped himself and looked up. His lips moved in silent poetry where silence rhymed with death.

It took him a few minutes to make it to the building, leaving everyone who saw him in disbelief, wondering what had happened to their straight-as-an-arrow CEO. They had no way of knowing what had happened.

Could he see their lips syncing, "Good Morning Mr. Waters" or see their elbows nudging each other in snarky insinuations? It's anyone's guess. Chuck, the Security Chief at the front desk, immediately called Katherine, C.W.'s Administrative Assistant, as the disheveled boss made his way to the elevator.

"Brace yourself Katherine. Looks like your boss tied one on last night. Yeah, he's a mess. Better get some coffee ready. He's gonna need it." Chuck snickered after he gently dropped the phone on the hook.

As C.W. got off the elevator, he walked past Katherine, who was waiting for him with a cup of coffee. She called after him as he walked by, ignoring her. "Your 9:00 A.M. Staff Meeting is ready for you, Mr. Waters." She followed him into the meeting room, pulled out his chair for him and stared at her memo pad as she recited the upcoming appointments he was going to have, not wanting to give away her shock at his appearance. He kept staring at the ceiling as he walked robotically to his chair. His staff had been waiting for almost twenty minutes. They had been chatting with each other while they waited, but lost their voices when C.W. entered the room.

He felt his way to his chair and sat down as if he had never sat in it before. He kept staring at the ceiling fan and mumbling to himself, acknowledging no one in the room. Two minutes of silence turned into three until Katherine re-entered the room to break the ice and hand out the meeting agendas to all the attendees.

She backed out of the room cautiously and shrugged her shoulders at the staff when C.W. giggled as he followed the blades of the rotating fan with his head. His giggling then became hysterical laughter. Tom Prentice, the CFO, sensing something terrible was about to happen, jumped up, went over to C.W. and tried to whisper some comforting words which didn't work. C.W. suddenly popped up out of his chair, violently shoved the CFO into a nearby wall, and left. He gave the group one last departing look with a contorted face, clenched jaw, and demon-looking eyes.

• • • •

THE FIERCE WINTER WIND in the parking lot defied the brilliant sunlight, pushing the CEO and making whipping sounds with his wrinkled untucked shirt. Bob was still warning the world that his door and windows were open, but no one was listening.

"Destination?"

The broken man didn't answer. He leaned as far back as he could in the plush leather. Bob closed his windows as C.W. almost fell asleep until Chuck started knocking on Bob's window. C.W. told Bob where to go.

"Shallow Pan."

"The Shallow Pan's operating hours are 6:00 p.m. to midnight."

"Shallow Pan."

• • • •

THE SHALLOW PAN WAS an old-fashioned Steak House on West Colfax. It was surviving, but almost at the end of its useful life. It lived on the corner of Fear the Beer (Dangerous Craft Beer) and Mama Funk's Fusion Soul food, another trendy Korean Taco food truck. Carleton Waters liked their steaks despite the trolling Mystery Munchers who'd been circling The Shallow Pan for years. Their scavenging ways didn't work, at least not for Waters. No matter how many one-star reviews came out, this restaurant that lived in a time capsule wasn't ready to be buried yet. But the mad comments kept coming:

"The steaks were tough," said Beefy Jim.

"Belligerent wait staff," cried Dainty Dianne.

"Too many red velvet curtains and oak-lined walls. Is this a magic show or a restaurant? The only thing missing were the robes and turbans and crystal balls," mocked Tasty Jane.

• • • •

TYLER HAD BEEN THE Pan's Head server for years. He somehow became the head server by outlasting or scaring off every other server over the past twelve years. He was the Commander-In-Chief of an army of four. And then there was Jordan, the eternally late-for-work Jordan. Four years of Tyler was usually as much as anyone could take, but Jordan was now in his fifth year.

As he brewed the coffee, Jordan made sure he added some extra emphasis to his hand-rubbing and blowing hot air into his fists. He knew he would need a little help, and in his mind, it would somehow help.

"Freakin' cold out there dude," said Jordan to Tyler, who was still massaging the same fork with the same dish towel since he'd started.

"Ok slacker, just finish the tables," commanded the leader.

"Should I sweep the floor first?" asked Jordan with that little puppy fear he was famous for.

"Did I say sweep or tables?" asked Tyler.

• • • •

• • • •

"PRIME TIME EVERYONE. Get your suck-up on and your noses up," said Tyler. Jordan cared little for Tyler's sarcasm, but he knew there was probably some truth in it, somewhere.

"Ten bucks C.W. shows up at 6:05 tonight," said Tyler. Then Jordan responded.

"How is that even a bet when you know he'll be here?"

"Not really, dude. The asshole hasn't been here for over a month," said Tyler, who had seen Bob at a far corner of the parking lot.

"I don't know, man; the old guy always shows up with his hot wife and out-of-control brat."

"Well, you never know. The old jerk might have croaked for all we know," said Tyler. "Haven't you heard everyone dies? Everyone dies, even C.W. I'm just giving you a chance to win some money dude, that's all. It's your choice if you want to throw away an opportunity to win some cash. That's your call. You know you're not getting a tip from him, right? He never tips. That's as sure as the fact that everyone dies," said Tyler. "And no second chances. Take it now or leave it." Tyler extended his hand to Jordan to consummate the bet.

"No thanks," Jordan said.

"Your loss, slacker, not mine!" finished Tyler.

It was fortunate for Jordan that he didn't take the bet because at exactly 6:05 p.m., older adult gentleman they referred to as C.W., walked into The Pan. No one knew his real name, but C.W. was what was monogrammed on every one of his expensive cuff-linked white shirts and he always paid in cash, as little cash as possible.

But something was different tonight. Why was he carrying a woman's coat draped over his left arm and why did he look like that?

Tyler had always been the best at handling C.W. Tyler knew that C.W. always needed some time to settle in. The old man always picked his own table, so Tyler watched him carefully from a distance, giving him enough time to place the coat gently over the back of the chair opposite him. C.W. gently pushed in the chair, leaving just enough room as if someone was sitting in it. From under the lady's coat, C.W. took out a small teddy bear — an older antique looking bear. He placed the bear on a chair to his right after holding it on his lap and then nuzzled it closer to the table. The night had closed in.

"Good evening, sir. Good to see you again. Will your guests be arriving shortly?"

Jordan stood there and waited.

"Can I bring you something to drink, sir?"

"Where's Brian?"

Good servers know how to punt; they say it's a gift. "I think today is his day off, sir."

He could tell that C.W. didn't hear a word.

The man's face was long and hard, like granite. Maybe time had turned it to stone. As he stared out into the parking lot, he started talking.

"Ok. We're ready. Oh, and please bring a child's menu. He's young but reads well for his age."

Jordan noted his requests and returned to the wait station.

"Having fun, slacker?" asked Tyler.

• • • •

LITTLE JENNY, TWO TABLES away from C.W., saw the Teddy Bear sitting peacefully in his chair. She fell in love with Mr. Ted as soon as she saw him. Jenny's parents were having an intense conversation and didn't notice that the little girl had walked towards Mr. Ted, and neither did C.W.

When you stare at ghosts in the rain, they all look the same. C.W. looked right through himself in the window as the trees flailed away at his apparitions. The silent raindrops also slid down his face.

As soon as Jordan placed the food on the table, C.W. realized that Mr. Ted was gone. Nothing could have prepared Jordan or anyone else for the scream of 'No' that came from somewhere deep inside the old man. That sound was like nothing he'd ever heard before. A sound like that could only mean a heart attack or unimaginable pain. Everyone rushed over to C.W. but didn't notice that little Jenny was gone.

Then Jenny's mother realized that her daughter wasn't there.

"Jenny, Jenny, where's my baby? Jenny!" She turned her head on a swivel and ran up to C.W., grabbing at his jacket and accusing him of something. "You, you, what did you do to my baby? I heard you scream at her. What did you do to her?"

The servers and the customers started looking everywhere. Jen's mother lifted C.W. out of his chair and dared him to answer. No one had ever stared him down like that before, but she did, and it meant something. The search was on.

She was nowhere to be found. Minutes felt like hours, then Jenny's mother opened the entry door to The Pan. The wind and rain crashed the door open, almost pulling it off its hinges. She ran out into the parking lot. The old man was right there with her when she found Jenny, soaking wet and clutching Mr. Ted. C.W. put his arms around both of them as they made their way back inside.

"Jenny, that Teddy Bear is not yours. Please give it back to this gentleman," said the relieved father.

The little girl lifted her right hand and held up Mr. Ted. Carlton Waters smiled at Jenny and said, "Mr. Ted asked me if he could go home with you. He's been with us for a long time, but he said he likes you and he hopes you will be his friend... will you?"

Jenny nodded softly and clutched the bear tightly. C.W. handed Jordan a hundred-dollar bill, took his wife's coat and walked out.

Bob opened his door for his passenger and was commanded by C.W. to call the Police. He gave Bob the number on Majeski's card.

• • • •

"I UNDERSTAND, SIR. Yes, yes," responded Majeski to the caller. He winked at Lonnie Jackson. "Yes, but we've completed our investigation," said the cop. "Yes, but what evidence do you have?"

Jackson could hear the voice on the other end because Majeski held out the phone.

"Sir, yes, I hear what you're saying. As soon as we get back on-duty we'll consider your 'feelings' about this and we'll definitely look into it. Yes." He winked again and clicked off his phone.

The older cop looked at the younger one and said, "He thinks he knows that his wife and son are alive."

"What makes him think that?" asked Jackson.

"Gut feeling," laughed the veteran cop.

"Grasping at straws?"

"You saw the remains. Did they look like they were alive to you?"

"Guess not."

• • • •

C.W. WASN'T USED TO being blown off.

"Bob, list every hospital in Denver that has an Emergency Room and an ICU. Then I want you to take me to each one."

"Calculating," said Bob.

The list of twenty hospitals appeared on the digital screen in alphabetical order, but C.W. wasn't a fan of the alphabet.

"Bob, don't drive to the hospitals in the order you've listed. I will tell you which ones to drive to and in what order. Go to Swedish first."

• • • •

C.W. TOOK OVER TO DRIVE. He would make the choices, and not the damn car. He had knocked three hospitals off the list, bribing ambulance drivers, and faking his own identity to ask who had been admitted. They drove. He gave it back to Bob.

"Stop! Stop, Bob," said C.W. "Stop in front of that church."

The Mother of God Catholic Church appeared in front of him and took him by surprise. Bob's wipers also stopped because the rain had stopped. The clearing evening sky revealed the most brilliant full moon that the old man had ever seen. He said a silent prayer that Bob couldn't hear and looked back at the list on the screen.

"Bob, take me to St. Joseph's Hospital and drive there as fast as you can."

"The average speed limit will be 45 Miles Per Hour."

"Override driving the damn speed limit or I'll do it myself. Go!"

"Overriding. Recalculating."

Bob did well, dodging double-parked cars, avoiding jaywalkers, and even driving through warning signals; red lights not so much. "Go through the red lights when it's clear," said C.W. He was even surprised that Bob got it.

• • • •

THERE WERE TWO AMBULANCES at the St. Joseph ER entrance. The drivers of both of them were leaning up against the first one. They were drinking coffee out of paper cups and half-listening to the two-way radio chatter. C.W. jumped out as Bob waited behind them at the entrance.

The taller one held up his paper cup at C.W. "Sir, you can't park there. You're blocking the entrance."

C.W. went over to Bob and told him to park himself in a parking space, which he did. The looks of amazement on the faces of the drivers meant nothing to C.W. "Have any of you brought in a woman and a child tonight?"

The older one took over with a, "Sir, patient privacy rules don't permit us to divulge any patient information." C.W. then flashed a hundred-dollar bill. "Sir, what you're doing is against the law."

"Look, my wife and child are missing. Something must have happened to them because I haven't heard from them or seen them. I know they're hurt somewhere. Please tell me if you've brought in a woman and a child? Don't you understand?"

The older driver was called away and had to leave in a hurry. The younger one looked around and asked C.W. to follow him into the parking lot. After looking around some more, he turned off his two-way radio. "A woman and child were brought in this evening. I saw them come in. Don't know if they're the ones you're looking for, but please don't tell anyone how you found out." He refused the hundred. C.W. ran into the hospital, ran to the ICU and surprised a nurse who had opened the doors with her badge. He ran in behind her and started looking into each room.

When Security was called to apprehend C.W., it didn't matter. He saw Jennifer and Brian and they were alive. C.W. went to the nursing station and told them who he was and wanted to know if Jen and Brian were going to make it. A matronly looking nurse told him that patient information was confidential and that he would have to leave. There was a nurse behind her who caught C.W.'s eye. She nodded at C.W. as if to say they were going to be ok.

While Security detained him, they told him that Jennifer and Brian were victims of a carjacking. They had been pistol whipped to where they almost died. The thieves took all of their money, cards, IDs and left them for dead except that a witness to the crime called 911. That witness, an older woman, accompanied the ambulance to the ER to stay with Jen and Brian.

The Police then came to arrest C.W. for trespassing. They couldn't figure out why he looked like the happiest man they'd ever arrested. C.W. thanked everyone he could see, including the good Samaritan, as he was led away in handcuffs.

"Another full moon and this one's for the books," said the cop.

C.W. couldn't stop smiling as he wondered if Majeski was still on duty.

Jimmy Stokes walked behind his fingers, pushing them on, and sliding them forward on the smooth surface of the kitchen counters. It felt flawless and cold; their edges sharp and waiting.

And now that it was over, a passing thought occurred to him. Maybe what happened never happened! What if it had been some kind of sick trick being played, a nightmare, or a payback? But when he heard the shadows rubbing against the walls... he knew. What had happened wasn't a misunderstanding. Then he remembered the phone call that changed everything.

It was Bryce, the manager at Pyros.

"Jimmy, Bryce down at Pyros... Hello, Jimmy, you there?" Jimmy saw 1:05 A.M. on his clock.

"Yeah, Jimmy here."

"Sorry to call you so late, bro, but my whole damn security system just went down in the middle of this big party down here. Can you come down ASAP and fix it for me? I really need your help so bad, bro, I really do."

Jimmy Stokes was the owner of 'Peace of Mind Security'. Late phone calls from clients were the price of doing business, but they were annoying. He cleared his throat to get the words out. "Alright man... just give me a few minutes." He could hear laughter behind Bryce.

"Thanks Jimmy. You're the best, bro."

"Yeah, yeah... sure..."

He threw on whatever he could find first; hoodie, shorts, and a Dallas Cowboy's cap to cover his messed up thinning brown hair. He smiled at himself in the bathroom mirror when he thought about the day Hil, his best friend Hilton Carlisle, gave him that hat on his eighteenth birthday. It was a throwback hat, and he appreciated it because it was from the Danny White days, which was his favorite cowboy era.

Those days were the best. He and Hil had grown up together since elementary school, and Hil knew him like a book. He gave himself one last look in the mirror and decided it didn't matter. Who cares how I look? Besides, Pyros is a gay bar?

The frigid evening air had some bite to it as he pulled into the parking lot at Pyros, still rubbing the sleep out of his eyes and yawning. His only thought was, just let me get this over with so I can go back home and go to sleep. When he turned off the engine, he could feel the pulsing disco music coming from inside the club.

The hug from Bryce was a little over the top, but since Pyros was a good client and Bryce was ok, Jimmy let it go. It didn't take him long to install a new hard drive, update the software, and delete a bunch of old security videos that weren't needed.

Viewing the last of those videos slammed his brain into a wall. He turned around to see if anyone was looking over his shoulder and ran it again. Bryce shrugged it off when he spotted Jimmy leaving in a hurry.

He sat in his car, stunned, as the rest of the cars in the parking lot laughed at him. He edged over to the rearview mirror to see what they were laughing at. When he saw what he saw, it scared the shit out of him.

Now there were cars everywhere, expensive cars — some between and some not between the lines. Getting out of there would not be easy, but he wanted out bad. Someone had parked in front of him, so the only way out was to go in reverse. The last car he passed by was a black Rolls Ghost. He knew what it was because one of the Cowboy's best pass rushers had one just like it.

Jimmy almost forgot he was going in reverse when he made it out of the parking lot and into the street, but an oncoming car blew its horn and jerked him back to reality. He clenched the steering wheel as hard as he could and put his forehead on it, in case his head fell off.

That damned video wouldn't stop playing repeatedly in his mind. They say, if it's not your time but you feel you might die, only the important moments in your life flash in front of you. There they were; Jimmy and Hil walking home from school and punching each other's arms, and again at Boy Scout camp. Their families also went to San Diego together, like they'd done so many times. And there they were on their pilgrimage to Cowboy Stadium, absolutely the best moment of his life, until the day he met Becky, Rebecca Masterson, his miracle. She was a receptionist at one of his clients.

The next day, Jimmy texted Hil. He didn't know what to do, so he took the easy way out, canceling their Super Bowl Watch Party and blaming it on Becky, with a lame excuse any six-year-old would have known was bullshit. Hil always answered any text, but this time he didn't. Later on, Jimmy met Becky for breakfast.

They walked into a local coffee shop together. Her long legs and thin body matched the fine features of her face. She was graceful and beautiful, and she loved Jimmy.

"I hope you don't mind, but I used you as my excuse to cancel our usual Super Bowl party. There's just no way I could act like everything was the same."

"No, that's ok," said Becky. She moved her hand towards Jimmy but stopped short. "Maybe a quick break for you guys will help. I don't know about you, but lately, when the three of us got together, it felt different. At first, I thought, maybe he didn't like me very much. But then I thought, well, maybe it was because we were spending too much time together and he thought he was being left out. I know how close you guys have been."

"I noticed nothing like that," said Jimmy.

Becky's eyes kept searching for a comfortable place to rest.

"I'm not sure. Maybe he's got something going on in his life. It's happened to me before and I was totally clueless about how I looked to other people. Then someone told me and I was literally shocked."

"I can't handle this, Becky. I really can't," said Jimmy.

Jimmy and Becky killed time for the rest of the day. They didn't talk much as Becky knew he was stuck when he told her he needed some time to think. She said she understood. After all, it wasn't as though the problem was another woman.

When Jimmy got home, he didn't realize how tired he was, so he slept and when he woke up, it was getting dark outside. Something, maybe a sound, startled him, causing him to be wide awake. There were a couple of texts from Hil and one from Becky, seeing if he was ok. He texted her back, but not Hil. Eventually, he replied to Hil's texts, but nothing came back. The morning appeared out of nowhere. He made a pot of coffee and turned on the local news.

Breaking news just coming in. Albuquerque Police were
called to the scene of an apparent suicide. There doesn't
appear to be any foul play involved, but for now, police
are not commenting on any of the details in this case
until their investigation is completed and relatives are notified.

He stopped to look out the window and into the parking lot, hoping to see Hil's car out there. Instead, he noticed what looked like the same black Rolls Ghost he'd seen at Pyros, but the windows were too dark to see inside.

Hil's car wasn't in the parking lot. As he propped his feet up on the coffee table and began his first cup of coffee, he realized the apartment complex where the suicide happened was Hil's. In fact, it was the same area as Hil's apartment. He turned off the T.V. and started making breakfast for himself.

Later, the T.V. was turned on again.

The Police have notified the immediate relatives of
the suicide victim. His name is Hilton Carlisle. More
details to follow.

He knew it before he heard the news. When two friends were as close as he and Hil, they were two copies of the same person. They know everything about each other. He shook his head so slightly that if anyone had been looking, they wouldn't have noticed.

The first thing he did was call Hil's parents. They'd become his own parents, especially after his mother died. It was like having a second set of parents that you could talk to when you needed to talk to someone bad. But they didn't answer his call and the entire day passed away. Jimmy looked at the Sandia Mountains from his patio and talked to them in a language he'd just made up, in case God was listening and needed some time to figure it out.

He jammed a magazine carelessly into a little wooden magazine rack and tossed a half-empty coffee cup into the sink, shattering it to pieces. As Wednesday evening crept up on him and the shadow of death covered the Sandias, Jimmy cramped himself inside out. He knew there were other names for sunsets, and death and bullshit, but he couldn't recall any of them at the moment.

The Rolls car in the parking lot was gone, but when he drove to Hil's parents' house, he saw it again at the end of their street. He had no idea what he was going to tell Mary and Bruce because he knew it wouldn't make any difference. He saw their cars parked in their driveway. They looked like two tombstones.

He knocked gently at first but they wouldn't respond. He knocked harder and then rang the doorbell. Once, wait, twice, wait, three times, stop. Their hidden faces were twisted, angry, and fuming.

When they saw Jimmy leave, because they wouldn't answer, Bruce Carlisle opened the front door, making Jimmy get out of his car and walk back. Bruce stared him down as he approached and when Jimmy made it to the door, Bruce said, "You did this! Never come back here ever again!" Mary was directly behind him as Bruce scorched Jimmy with his eyes. She had a different look. It looked like anger, but it wasn't.

As he walked back to his car, Mary followed him. Bruce tried to hold her back, but she had something to say to Jimmy and she was not to be denied. When she caught up with him by his car, her eyes kept looking toward the Rolls.

"You were his best friend. His best friend. He needed you. Why didn't you help him?"

"I was pissed that he never told me he was gay. I found out by accident and he never told me."

"That's why you turned your back on him?" Mary's eyes were still focused on the black Rolls.

Jimmy had no answer for Mary, at least none that he will admit to, so he left her in the driveway. The grief he felt overwhelmed him as he sped past the Rolls. He stopped and backed up next to it, trying to see inside its blackness. It slowly and silently pulled away, leaving Jimmy behind. When he looked in his rearview mirror, Mary was still standing in her driveway, staring at him. He wanted to tell her in the worst way why he'd turned his back on his best friend, not that it mattered. They both knew.

• • • •

JIMMY'S PHONE RANG. It was Nora, his grandmother. When he was fifteen, his mother had suddenly passed away, and Nora had offered to help. Jimmy's father never cared for Nora, so he kept their get together to a minimum. Sometimes Jimmy visited Nora without telling his father. Not that he needed a new mother; it was just that sometimes being in the presence of an older woman felt good, even though men never admitted stuff like that.

It just dawned on him it was the first Wednesday of the month. They always had dinner on the first Wednesday and he realized that this was her usual reminder.

"Don't worry Grandma, I'll be there. Don't worry."

Nora waved him over to her table, but when he sat down, nothing happened. He couldn't hear anything she was saying. She kept on talking and while her lips moved, all Jimmy could see was Hil laughing and rolling on the floor and dancing like a cheerleader, kicking his leg up in the air, doing a split, and breaking into two pieces and...

"Oh, and tell me Jimmy, how's Becky? You know God smiled at you when you found that beautiful girl..."

"Why would he smile at me if he let me do that to Hil?" Jimmy's voice boomed across the restaurant as his fist came down forcefully on the table. He leaned across to Nora with his eyes almost bulging out of his head. "HOW COME?"

Nora wasn't scared, but she was embarrassed. She seemed to be more concerned with the patrons leaving the restaurant and the looks on their faces. But all was well when she noticed a calm and very handsome bald-headed gentleman seated by a window who kept eating his meal as if nothing had happened. Nora touched her hair, as women do, when appearances matter.

"Now don't go blaming yourself for..."

Jimmy sprang up out of his chair and knocked everything off the table. "Oh, don't you worry about that, grandma! God's already taken care of that for me."

Nora took off to the parking lot. The manager approached Jimmy but backed off when she saw the twist of anger in his face; it was too much. Jimmy megaphoned the rest of his speech to the almost, except for the well-dressed bald man eating his meal, empty restaurant.

"Doesn't anybody give a shit about anybody anymore? How do you look at yourself in the mirror and actually say you're a human being when you turn on someone you love for no reason, no fucking reason at all? Tell me. How does that happen?" Jimmy stopped for a second, then pointed at the bald man eating. "Hey you, bald man. You. Stop eating and look at me. Hey!"

The man kept eating. Jimmy's long, threatening strides ended at the bald man's table. The manager had just gotten off the phone with the police and she looked scared.

The man dabbed at the corners of his mouth with his napkin and, with an open palm, invited Jimmy to have a seat. "Please, sit."

"I don't want to sit!" Jimmy said throwing the empty chair across the dining room. "I want you to answer my question."

"In due time, but first, I'd much prefer to finish this lovely Caprese Salad first, before it wilts. You don't mind, do you?"

"How the fuck do you know me because I sure as shit don't know you?"

"I probably know more about you than you know about yourself."

"How?" Jimmy swiped the man's entire meal on the floor, bent over and came close enough to almost touch noses.

"Hilton told me. Lovers talk, you know. Well, maybe you don't know, but then again, maybe you do."

"Who are you?"

The man pulled out a revolver from under his belt and pointed it at Jimmy. "Actually, my plan was to kill you, just like I killed Hilton. But after I heard your little speech a while ago, I... Who am I? That's an excellent question indeed. Let's start with my name. I'm Sterling Chalmers and I've been Hilton's lover for almost five years now. That's right Jimmy. Hilton was gay, a fact that I'm sure comes as a great surprise to you."

The gun that was pointed at Jimmy calmed him down. "You said you killed Hil. Why?"

"It's quite simple. After five years of hearing your name repeatedly, and how much he loved you and how he could never ever love another man but you, Jimmy, well, I got so sick of hearing it..." The flashing lights and Police sirens punctuated the standoff. "Hilton was in unbearable pain because of you and Becky. I simply put him out of his misery." Chalmers nodded in self-approval. "It seemed like the right thing to do."

Sterling Chalmers dropped his gun when the Police stormed in and he was quickly handcuffed. They asked him if he was Sterling Chalmers and if he was the one who murdered Hilton Carlisle? He said yes to both questions.

While walking out under arrest, he turned to Jimmy and said, "Jimmy, Hilton really loved you. And after hearing your speech tonight, I knew that you really loved him in your own way."

It might have been an hour or it might have been a lifetime, but they eventually impounded the Ghost. Nora hugged her Jimmy and Jimmy patted her gently on her back. Nothing changes in the dark, the place where shadows laugh at fools.

Tony's Last Grandma

His passenger was an attractive brunette, and she was friendly enough. So, the Brooklyn cabbie took his time, kept turning around to talk to her as he drove with one hand going south on Flatbush. A loud thud on his right front fender broke his fantasy, causing him to slam his brakes!

• • • •

WHAT HE COULDN'T HAVE known, because he wasn't paying attention, was that an eighteen-year-old street operator named Anthony Salvatore Cantoro, 'Tony Cannoli' to the local cops, had been watching him from his favorite lamp post. He'd been smoking a cigarette and savoring a freshly baked cannoli, when, in a flash, his instincts took over. In less than ten seconds, he fell to the ground, moaning and groaning and scanning, with one eye in control.

• • • •

THE BRUNETTE BOLTED, and the cabbie threw a twenty at Tony after he whispered something in his ear. Tony hobbled his way to the curb and in one smooth motion, slid the twenty into his pants pocket and rubbed his rib cage.

A murmuring crowd of entertained pedestrians gathered as Barney Stillman, the local cop on the beat, approached the scene from around the corner. Myra Levant, a window-shopping widow, had witnessed the entire event. But when Stillman kicked Tony and told him to get his lazy ass up and move along, the widow reacted.

She pointed her trembling cane at Tony.

"Can't you see the young man's hurt, officer?"

"He's a con artist lady. Believe me, he does this all the time."

Tony lifted himself up gingerly, as the prospect of a new and more appealing opportunity glowed with possibilities.

"Put your hand on my shoulder, young man, and walk home with me. I'll get you fixed up," said Myra.

"It's ok, I'll be all right."

"Nonsense, young man, you come right along with me, I insist."

The disappointed gawkers continued throwing their chins at the diminutive widow and the handsome, tall teen with his hand on her shoulder. All Stillman could do was to shake his head and tell the chin throwers to be on their way.

• • • •

TONY'S EYES WERE ALWAYS working overtime, even more so now, as Myra fumbled for the keys in her purse. It took her a while, but as she unlocked and opened the creaking door, she pointed her cane at an old recliner by a window.

"Now, you just sit there in George's recliner. I know he'd like that very much. Go ahead."

Myra dusted her curios with a feather duster that had also seen better days.

"Who's George?" asked Tony.

"Oh, I'm sure you mean my late husband, George? He was a science teacher at Erasmus High School and a good man. Yes, he was."

"You wouldn't have a beer, would you? I could use one, Grandma."

As he talked, Tony scanned everything in the apartment. The curios and knickknacks lining the walls caught his attention. I could grab a few and be gone and she wouldn't even know it.

But something else distracted him. What it was and how to handle it was different. Maybe it was that smell. The smell of old age was everywhere, and it made him uncomfortable.

"I think the best thing for you right now would be... what did you say your name was young man?... Are you sure you're my grandson?"

"Tony."

"Tony. The best thing for you right now would be a nice cup of hot tea. It will make you feel so much better and it won't take but a minute to fix." Myra walked towards the kitchen, but paused. "Do you go to Erasmus High School, Timmy?"

"My pop told me to quit all that school shit and get a job. Besides, I like the good things in life." He flashed his jewelry at the old lady, "Which is why I'm self-employed, if you know what I mean."

"When was the last time you talked to your father?"

"Look Grandma, how 'bout that cup of tea? I'm feeling a little dizzy," he said, touching his forehead and closing his eyes.

By the time she returned, Tony and a half dozen of her knickknacks were gone.

Tony walked a little slower than usual as he made his way back to Flatbush Avenue. The more he thought about it, the more the whole thing felt a little too easy. He liked the widow more than he liked what he did. But it was time to get back to work. Besides, she asked too many questions, anyway.

The next day, Tony had stationed himself on his favorite street corner, looking for income. Nothing was happening, and he was about ready to leave when he saw Myra walk into a second-hand shop across the street. But instead of leaving, he watched her from behind his personal lamppost.

· · · ·

IT DIDN'T TAKE LONG for her to leave, holding the same crystal pillbox that Tony had just sold to the store owner not twenty minutes earlier. Myra had taken it without paying, and the owner came running after her. He grabbed her by her arm and told her she had to pay for it or he would call the cops.

"Why should I pay for something that belongs to me?" said Myra.

"Because it's not yours, that's why?"

A small crowd gathered around the old woman and the shop owner. Their patience paid off when Officer Barney Stillman arrived. Tony also watched the drama unfold.

"She stole it. That's what she did, officer. She came in here, pretty as you please, walked over to the shelf with all the curios on it, and walked off with this pillbox without paying for it."

"You again? What's your name, lady?" asked the cop.

"I think they call me Grandma, Officer," the little group of shoppers laughed, "but I don't think it's my full name."

"What's your full name?"

"Well, at the moment, I can't seem to remember. But if you give me a second..."

The cop asked Myra if she took the small box. She emphatically said that it was hers and that she did not know how it got in his shop and that she was just taking what belonged to her.

Anthony Salvatore Cantoro looked worried, but not enough to get involved, yet. Business was business, and it was getting late. The frustrated shop owner was getting angrier, the cop more frustrated, and Myra, well, she couldn't figure out what was going on. There seemed to be no end to the unfolding drama.

"Lady," said the cop, "you took this from his store. He said you didn't pay for it. If you would just pay for it, this whole thing will be over. Can't you just pay for it so that we can be done here?"

"Oh yes, I can pay for it. But I won't because it belongs to me. That's just silly, officer," Myra said, smiling.

She grabbed the box out of the cop's hand and clutched it to her breast. He tried to take it back, but Myra wouldn't let go. Tony had now seen enough. He had a gnawing feeling in his gut and it wasn't from too many cannolis.

Traffic on Flatbush was heavy, but he knew he had to fix Myra's problem. Tony was a masterful jaywalker; he walked through the congestion of cars like a ballet dancer. It was a sight to see. The cop didn't see him saunter over, but when he did, his eyes automatically rolled.

"Stay out of this Tony," said Stillman.

"I'm telling you, I can settle this whole misunderstanding. I saw the whole thing from across the street and I can tell you exactly what happened."

"Stay out of it. I don't need your help. Now, back off."

When Tony resisted, the cop lost his cool.

"Back off now, or you're going to jail with her." Stillman's neck was throbbing. "You hear me?"

Tony wouldn't budge. And when the cop decided that he'd had enough of the both of them, he grabbed Tony and tried to put handcuffs on him.

"Stop that, officer! I think he's my grandson. Stop it! Can't you see that you're hurting him?"

"Enough Lady. I've had it with both of you."

But Myra was adamant. She poked the police officer with her cane and he grabbed her arm while still trying to cuff Mr. Cannoli. Then the crowd edged in as this was getting good. Myra seemed to sway public opinion. Someone in the crowd yelled, "Leave the old lady alone!"

The cop put the cuffs on Tony and put another set on Myra, but stopped himself. He bent over to talk to the diminutive widow.

"Look Lady. I have to do this. You can't go around poking police officers with your cane. If you promise to behave yourself, I won't put the cuffs on you. Will you behave yourself?"

"I am behaving myself. It's you that isn't behaving himself," responded Myra as she poked the cop once again with the cane.

"Ok, that's it."

The cop put Myra in cuffs and called for a wagon. He gave the shop owner the crystal Pill Box and the Police van arrived.

"You don't have the right to give him my property," said the widow.

The cuffs were taken off of Myra and Tony. The rollicking van jolted them in different directions as it sped off. They sat opposite each other and said little. Myra almost fell over when they turned a corner at a high speed. Tony waited for Myra to say something, but she ignored him strangely. She simply smiled at him as if she'd just met a stranger and was offering a polite smile as a courtesy.

"Grandma, don't you remember me? I went to your home, and you showed me your collections and you made me a cup of tea. Remember?" Myra didn't answer. Her eyes just wandered all around the Police van.

"Come on, don't you remember me? You asked me about my dad and if I went to Erasmus High School. You liked me. You thought I was your grandson."

"Are you my grandson?" Tony couldn't answer. "Can you believe they'd arrest an old lady like me? I'm not a criminal. Well, I don't think I am. Am I...what did you say your name was?"

"Tony. Tony Cannoli, I'm..." Tony stopped himself, searching every inch of her face.

"Phillip, do you think I'll be going to jail?"

Tony reached across and held her hand. She smiled at the stranger in front of her. The van smelled of booze and vomit from the previous inhabitants and rocked back and forth on its journey.

"Look Grandma, this is all my fault. If I hadn't done what I did, we wouldn't be here and none of this would have happened. I shouldn't have done it. That's all."

As the van approached the Police station, it came to a sudden stop. Tony made sure that Myra wouldn't fall over by putting his hand on her shoulder and keeping her in place. She smiled warmly at the young man.

The two troublemakers were escorted into the police station. A veteran cop saw the group walk in and he shook his head.

"Well, Stillman, looks like you caught yourself a couple of real bad ones there."

"Shut up Tim. Where's Sargent Donahue?"

"Eating his lunch. But if you want me to disturb him so these killers won't hurt anyone else, I'd be glad to do that. I mean, they look pretty dangerous."

Tony used to appreciate sarcasm wherever it came from. But it didn't sound the same. He stayed close to Myra as they sat on a bench waiting for the Sargent to finish his lunch.

He held her hand while they waited, and his eyes remained fixed on hers.

"You ok Grandma?" whispered Tony into her ear.

"Certainly, young man. These police officers are so nice, aren't they? And what they do for all of us is so important. They keep us safe, you know."

"I know."

For Tony, a very unusual idea was forming in his mind. Tell the cops the truth!

"You again Cantoro?" asked Sgt. Donahue.

"I can explain everything."

"How many grandmas does this one make? Twenty, thirty, a hundred? Seems to me you'd be bored by now."

"I know. But if you'll just listen to me for one second, there's a simple explanation for all of this."

The Sargent picked at his teeth with a toothpick and walked away.

A few hours passed by and Myra was released. Tony waved goodbye to Myra, but only after she left. He was released with the usual warning to knock it off or else, which made sense to him now.

Two months had passed since Tony and Myra went their separate ways. His plan to return to school, buy back the crystal pillbox, return it to Myra, and to talk to his dad after all those years on the street was well under way. Everything was rolling along perfectly and, to Tony's surprise, it felt good.

The very first thing he did was buy back the pillbox, because he figured somebody would buy it and he'd be out of luck. Mordie, the shop owner, recognized Tony and asked him what he was looking for, even though he knew.

"The thing that caused it, the little box," said Tony as he perused the curios. "I don't see it. Did somebody buy it already?"

The proprietor curled his finger at the teen, and they walked toward the back of the store. "Wait here." He came back with the curio in his hand and Tony smiled. That meant more than simple gratitude, and the shop owner recognized it immediately.

They walked back to the register and when Tony asked "how much", the man gave him the thumb to leave. Tony tried to leave a ten-dollar bill, but the man refused to take it and smiled toward the door.

The going back to school part of his plan was not as easy as he thought. First, he'd been out of school for so long that the Guidance Counsel at Erasmus High School told him he'd be the oldest freshman they'd ever had and that his police record was worrisome. "You're not exactly the kid that would be a positive influence on these young kids just coming in to High School."

Tony assured him of his good intentions. "On the contrary. I'd be the perfect influence on them."

"How so?"

"Because if I saw a kid going in the wrong direction like I did, I'd set him straight and they'd know I'd be telling them the truth. Sometimes, that's all a kid needs. Am I right?"

The Counselor stared at Tony with a wry smile that hinted good things to come. "Ok Tony, call me tomorrow and I'll let you know what we've decided."

They shook hands and made eye contact. Tony had a good feeling when he walked alone on Flatbush. He'd seen all of it before, but it looked different that day.

• • • •

HIS TWO ROOMMATES COULDN'T figure out what was happening to Tony. He'd ditched his mafia clothes, his cigarettes and his cannoli. He figured it was time to give Myra back her crystal pillbox, which he had carefully gift-wrapped with heart-covered wrapping paper and a pink ribbon.

The sign on the front of Myra's building said, 'Apartment for rent. See building superintendent in Apartment 1 C.' Tony didn't give it much thought as he walked up to Myra's apartment. There was a 'For Rent' sign on her door, but he knocked anyway. He kept knocking harder and harder until the man next door came out to see who was making the racket. He was in his boxer shorts and undershirt and was smoking the last of the stub of his cigar.

"If you're looking for the old lady, she ain't here no more."

"Where is she?" asked Tony.

"Nowhere. You a relative?"

"Yes, I'm her grandson." Tony didn't like what he just said, but he needed to find out what happened to Myra. "Now, can you please tell me where she is?"

"The old lady died about a month ago, not too long after she got into trouble with the cops." The old man chewed his stogie for a second, then removed it as if he was about to say something important and he wanted to make sure the words came out right. He could see that the news hit Tony hard.

"I knew her and her husband George for a long time. They were both good people, always helping kids who needed help, you know, just good people. But people talk when they should keep their mouths shut and a lot of the people who live here should have kept their mouths shut. They said stuff to her that never should have been said. I guess it was too much for her."

. . . .

FROM THAT POINT ON, everything Tony did, he did in honor of Myra. And when he called the Counselor at Erasmus High, and was told that he could come back to school, he thanked the man and told him he wouldn't be sorry. The man told him he knew he wouldn't be and to report to class the next day.

But that wasn't the end of Tony's story, not by a long shot.

. . . .

ANY TIME HE THOUGHT about Myra in his later years, Anthony Salvatore Cantoro, now a prominent Brooklyn attorney, always blew a kiss to her in heaven; that special place where our angels keep their eyes on us, no matter what we've done.

Music for Simana

Washington DC, June 22, 2018.

The concert began at midnight. It felt as though music was pouring down from the stars. The music felt like lavender feels when you walk through a field in the spring. All the constellations glistened in the moonlight, and Jillian's doubts and premonitions disappeared; she was home now.

Something moved as she harvested the last of the garden sounds, and then she was finished.

She heard critical interpretations from the milling crowd, clanking silver spoons dipped in bullshit, feeding them and tricking them into believing they appreciated something they knew nothing about.

Time lapsed and Jillian was an orphan again.

Softly, as she rose, she contemplated her imminent reverse suicide. A rebirth in Maine amid the emerald green splendor and mirrors of beauty that you can't really see but know because and only because you've given up and tossed away an older piece of truth.

Rhythms are beat sequences that are disposable, like the ones left on the surrounding ground. She left them in disarray, telling her mother that in case she was wondering, she really loved her and that she wouldn't embarrass her anymore with her foolish ways.

This was unbreakable, this love, so it didn't matter what she did or said because reading her mind with poetry took magic.

A slow silence comes with dreams. You leave yourself alone to command the surrounding beauty, to embrace fire with fearless innocence.

• • • •

THERE IS A MAPLE TREE in the Maine woods that had been abused by humans for hundreds of years and cried to Jillian every night.

The pain she felt was too much. The tree said her name was Simana, and Jillian cried in reverence.

Mom told me to save you the best I could, so the least I could do was to come to you, be with you and protect you when you needed me, whether anything I've ever done came close to the truth. I will now be your guardian and don't worry, I won't let them hurt you again as much as I can and if I spill my blood on the ground around you as you reach for the sky and the earth, it will be my nourishment for you which isn't much but I love you, Simana.

Jillian arrived and found Simana weeping in pain. Her brothers and sisters were also crying. It was night, and the stars were overseeing and under darkness, apparently not listening, but Mom was.

Jillian tied herself to Simana in the dead of winter. There in the woods, she told Simana not to worry anymore because she was there now and the other trees cried with happiness as the Maine Woods felt safe in her presence and her death became music for the living.

Greed Doesn't Count

O k, I'll admit it, I'm a bottom feeder. And because of that, my name means nothing. I feed in the black water aquarium of cyber security. Bits and pieces are always dropping to me from the bigger predators. So, I make a decent living. Of course, the word 'living' isn't exactly what most people would call it. If you're so inclined, you can survive.

Baker James, his most recent name and the biggest predator of all, could have invented the Black Web even though he probably didn't. He lived so freely in it that if he didn't invent it, he should have, because nobody did it better. I say did it better, because I'm not even sure if he's still alive.

The vignette I'm about to tell you is a product of many retellings among those of us who live in this place. It's been patched together, taken apart, and reformatted so many times that some of it, all of it, or none of it may be true.

I can't tell you who I am or why I'm telling you this story. But I can tell you that none of us have names because not only is it unnecessary, it's damn dangerous. Whoever you are and whatever you do down here, you better not do it for very long because this place won't let you. Survival only happens by constant reinvention and, as we all know, reinvention can often bring with it many unforeseen consequences.

Take Baker James, for instance.

• • • •

THIS STORY STARTS EARLY on a rainy day in mid-September, in a recent year. It was early in the day for most people, but not for him. The call had to be made because the idiot left him no choice, and Sanja Kazimir knew it as soon as he got it. He knew he'd screwed up as he stared wide-eyed at his phone that lit up like an electric chair light bulb.

As soon as he answered it, his last call, the front door of his apartment flew open and in walked two 'Auditors'.

Baker James ended the call without a word and continued to trim his perfect stubble, staring out of his third-floor window to the street below. A homeless woman and her child were panhandling on the corner as light rain fell. His grooming was finished, but the buzz of the electric razor continued. He then carefully measured the length of his stubble with his thumb and forefinger.

His daily schedule comprised schemes with numbers attached to them. Some of them were whole numbers, some had decimals, and all of them were options. Because he knew how important it was to stay on the move and be invisible, wherever he stayed for the day or night, it wasn't a location to him; it was just a number.

It was 1.2 of 2 or less in today's apartment scheme—and it felt like it—so out came another phone from his suitcase. The thought of calling his bride-to-be Morgan Shapiro crossed his mind briefly. He knew she was waiting for his call because she thought she loved him, even though love had nothing to do with it. For Baker, it was all about possibilities and nothing else. 'Don't call her', was option #6. He smiled at his reflection in the window and turned away to get dressed. But something made him stop and look back at the street. The woman and the child had vanished, and Baker lost his smile. He didn't realize that he'd turned off the razor.

• • • •

THE RAIN STOPPED, AND the air smelled sweet, amid the street awnings dripping their finals on the soaked sidewalks below. When he walked down the service steps of 1.2, Baker scanned everything as he stepped out onto the pavement. He knew how and why he was being followed because the reason was always the same.

The guy with the camera on the fifth floor of the abandoned warehouse across the street was still there. The phony construction worker was still sweeping invisible debris, and the woman dressed as a parking cop was still putting fake tickets on cars. No matter, he had two Ubers ready, going in two different directions. He could lose the guy reading a newspaper in the black SUV by picking the Uber that went in the opposite direction. He even knew how to lose them, the best route to take, and just how fast to drive to get to apartment 2.0.

The attractive brunette driving the Uber he had chosen looked back at Baker and fell into the same trance every other woman fell into when they saw him. He was a man, unlike all the others; six feet four inches, wiry-framed, wavy black hair, facial features that didn't look real, perfect stubble beard, and the intense crystal blue eyes that refused to blink. They were all part of his spell-making machinery. He pulled out a crisp hundred and held it close to her face.

"If you get me to 746 Lamont St. in less than two minutes, this is yours," said Baker. "If you don't, you get nothing. Deal?"

"Anything you say Mr. St. John."

The screeching tires whined against the black wet asphalt. They made it to Lamont Street in just under three minutes. At first, Baker folded the hundred and motioned to put it back into his suit pocket. She also handed him a card with her phone number. He handed her the hundred and told her to get lost, fast. She sped up without looking, because she was still gawking at him. He tore her phone number into pieces and dropped it in a sewer as he walked to car #2.

The '85 peach-colored Corolla was 'clean'. Baker looked around one last time and drove to Apartment 2.0 to change and take car #3 to his Engagement Party. The air was dry because the sun had taken over, like it usually did in Montauk, in May.

There they were, again. The same woman and child were now in front of the Apartment Building of Apartment 2.0.

He parked the Corolla in front of a fire hydrant so that it would be towed away. Apartment 2.0 was around the corner, not on Lamont St.

Again, the woman and her child vanished. Baker stopped, looked up at
the clearing sky, and closed his eyes.

• • • •

THE TWENTY-FOOT TALL bay window of Marvin Shapiro's
Office looked out over acres of manicured lawns, a nine-hole golf
course, and an Olympic-sized swimming pool that had been carved out
of Italian marble by artisans, in Naples no less. It was 9 A.M., Saturday,
the 8th of May, the day of his daughter Morgan's engagement party.

There were mirrors everywhere but it didn't matter where he was
as long as he could see himself. He was wearing his trademark full
length maroon Japanese silk robe that he left wide open. It covered his
fat naked body as he viewed his estate. If anyone was looking at him,
well, that was their good fortune, which was Marvin's sole gesture of
benevolence to the world.

Jonas, the long-time butler at the Shapiro estate, knocked on
Marvin's half-opened office door, causing the 'Philanthropist' to turn
around. His silk robe was still wide open, revealing what he thought
was something magnificent, but it wasn't. It was fat, wrinkled, and
discolored. Jonas had seen it all before, so he ignored it.

"Your 9 A.M. appointment has arrived, sir."

"About damn time."

"Yes sir, shall I show him in, sir?"

"Oh yes, yes, please do. Bring him in, by all means." Marvin flapped
his hand in the air as he once again looked at himself in the mirror on
his large oak desk.

Blake Thompson, Chief Investigator for Black Light, Inc., came in
holding a very thin-looking file folder. He had come to this meeting
knowing he had nothing, but he came anyway.

The old man stared at him for what seemed like hours before he
said something. His full-frontal had no effect on the Detective who
waited for his client to speak.

"I'm curious Mr. Thompson. Do I look like a schmuck?"

Thompson knew better than to answer any question at that moment.

"I take your silence as a 'yes', in which case I have to ask that if I am a schmuck, which I'm not, can a schmuck have all this?" The billionaire's open hand pointed at his estate. "Of course not, Mr. Thompson, of course not. But stay with me on this, Mr. Thompson. If we agree that I'm not a schmuck, then you must be trying to make me look like a schmuck. Isn't that right, Mr. Thompson?"

The hard-nosed investigator had enough and answered. "No, Mr. Shapiro, we're not trying to make you look like a schmuck."

"Then why, Mr. Thompson, do I feel like a schmuck? Please tell me because I'm curious," asked Shapiro.

"We've looked everywhere, Mr. Shapiro, and I mean everywhere. Believe me when I tell you there's nothing."

"Mr. Thompson, I don't believe you. Why? Because we both know that's impossible. It's bad enough that I have to pay through the nose for this, but now, because you say it, I'm supposed to believe this bullshit. Come now Mr. Thompson."

"Look, Mr. Shapiro, you can believe whatever you want. The facts are that Baker James appeared. Call it out of thin air or whatever you want to call it, three years ago. There's nothing before that anywhere. But what I can tell you is that he's been a model citizen ever since, at least as far as we can determine. He's a successful executive of something, some kind of high-tech security firm. We're sure he makes a lot of money, and if you ask me whether your daughter caught herself a good one, I'd say definitely, and she's lucky to have him! Oh, and if you want us to return your retainer, we're more than happy to do that right now. We don't like to fail if you call this a failure."

"That's exactly what I call it and no, I don't want my money back. What I want are results!" said Marvin.

"Those are the results, Mr. Shapiro. Good day, sir." He dropped the file on the large desk.

As Thompson was leaving, Marvin raised his voice at him, saying, "What am I supposed to do now? The Engagement Party is in three hours. What am I supposed to do?" Marvin was now yelling at the detective, who made it to the front door of the mansion. "The guests are arriving. Everything has been arranged. What am I supposed to do now?"

Thompson stopped at the front door, turned around as he opened it and yelled back at the old man.

"You're supposed to enjoy it, Mr. Shapiro," he said, slamming the front door to the mansion as hard as he could.

Marvin also slammed his office door to show his anger was just as good as Thompson's. He felt good enough to smile at himself in the closest mirror.

"Who needs a fucking pacemaker when you're surrounded by idiots?"

"That's exactly what I tell myself all the time, Marvin." Suddenly, Baker James appeared out of nowhere right behind the smiling, now frowning billionaire.

"How about a nice massage, Marv, or should I say, Dad?"

His grip on Marvin's shoulders was so tight that the squirming old man couldn't move. "Relax Marv. Life's too short, especially yours. You should take Thompson's advice and enjoy it. These days don't come around very often, you know. There, feel better now?"

Baker ended the massage and walked over to Marvin's desk, helping himself to one of his Gurkha Black Dragons. Then, out came a tight roll of thousand-dollar bills. He carefully peeled away one of them and lit it with Shapiro's solid gold lighter. The fake smile and then playful frown on Baker's face mocked the ashen end of Grover Cleveland's face.

Marvin looked at his son-in-law-to-be with a wry smile of contempt and waited for him to say what he wanted to say. The glowing

Black Dragon consumed itself like a slow fuse. Baker blew large smoke rings in the air that wafted over the billionaire. The misty halos hovered over Marvin's bald head and drifted down in smokey veils.

As he approached Marvin, the difference in stature was embarrassing. The young upstart exhaled one last puff of valuable smoke into Marvin's face and dropped the stogie on the Persian Carpet. Then, a soft knock on the office door interrupted the contest.

"Dad, you decent?" said Morgan Shapiro as she entered her father's lair. "Hurry dad, the party's..."

"Babe!" Morgan looked shocked to see her father and her fiancé together. "I didn't know you were here."

"Hi babe, sorry. I wanted to ask for your father's permission. It's important to me, old-fashioned, I guess. So, today I asked his permission to marry you and he not only gave it to me, but we smoked cigars on it. We're BFFs now, babe. How cool is that?"

Morgan looked at her half-naked, full-frontal father and said, "Dad, close your robe, for God's sake. Please."

Marvin closed his robe and took in a deep breath. "Why don't the two of you go check on your Mother? I know she's all stressed out about today. I've got a few things to take care of before I get ready for the big day. Go ahead." As he urged the two to leave, he stopped as though he forgot something. "Oh, Morgan, can you let me have my future son-in-law for one more minute, please? I'll make sure you'll have him all to yourself?"

"Ok, but just one minute. That's all you get. I want him all to myself." Morgan left the two and closed the door. "Remember, one minute, that's it."

"I'll give you one thing, Mr. James. You're clever... but I think you're too clever for your own good. Don't think for a minute that you're going to get away with any of this. You'll never see a penny of mine. I guarantee it."

Baker took out a disposable smartphone and walked over to Marvin. As he towered over his future father-in-law, he shared the image on the screen with him. "I'm not interested in your pennies, Marvin. But I hope this will prove the sincerity of my intentions. I love your daughter and I will take excellent care of her." The image on his phone showed a voluntary transfer from Marvin to Baker of ten million dollars from one of Marvin's many secret offshore accounts. "I want you to know, Marvin, how much I appreciate this engagement gift. But you need to be a little more circumspect in your appreciation of your future son-in-law," said Baker, as he put his right arm around Marvin's shoulder. "Remember, we're BFFs now." Baker chuckled to himself, patted the old man on his butt, and kissed the top of his head as he walked out of the office.

He wasn't a big fan of paying to get money. The payment was making him believe he was in love with the bitch, as the thought of marrying her made him sick. But then, of course, there was the money.

He could deal with her later. Morgan gripped his hand like she was holding a piece of her favorite candy. She attempted to show him all the party preparations. He released his hand by fixing his tie, which was already fixed and smoothing his hair, which never fell out of place.

Kazimir's screw-up was stupid. Marrying the brat was simply the best of the lowest hanging fruit available.

Compared to everything else he did, this game was tedious. He knew all about Marvin's shell charities and conferences that were supposed to save the planet. He'd seen and temporarily rationalized Morgan's insatiable lifestyle and Millie's alcoholic rampages.

And then there was Millie's wine cellar. It was Marvin's gift to her on their 35th wedding anniversary. It had its own elevator and well over 12,000 bottles of the finest wines from all over the world. Millie lived in her wine cellar; she even had her own bedroom down there, which was fine with everyone who had to deal with her. It's better to let the ant live in a mountain of sugar than in the house.

It wasn't long before the elevator regurgitated its drunk. The elevator music was always Streisand because Millie said she sang like an angel and that one day she would meet her angel in heaven. 'Don't Rain on My Parade' from Funny Girl finished playing with its own applause. Baker remembered she had once told him she was a funny girl herself.

The brat ran over to her mother and tried to drag Baker with her. He had none of it, keeping himself in a far corner of the room while Millie commanded her servants to gather around her.

"Get over here, all of you," yelled Millie. "Look at this place. This should have been finished hours ago and you're all walking around here like you've got all day."

'The Help' reached the drunk before she ended her warning with, "You've got one hour to get all this finished. Get your lazy asses moving before I fire all of you and do it myself." All the blood left his face as Baker spotted something he could never have predicted.

This time, he grabbed Morgan's hand and walked with her toward the patio.

"You ok babe?"

"Yeah, just a migraine, that's all. All I need is a little fresh air and I'll be fine." As he pulled his bride-to-be with him, she looked like a reluctant little girl being pulled by her parent. Her stuttering footsteps matched her willing unwillingness. This was new to her and Baker could feel her curiosity peaking and had options already in place. They were now alone on the patio. He knew she had the nerve to ask stupid questions, so he patiently waited.

"Babe, why are we out here?"

"You are so amazing and you know me so well, babe. That's why I love you so much. Ok, you saw right through me, I'll admit it. I had an ulterior motive to get you out here. You got me. All I wanted was a quiet spot away from everyone to tell you how much I love you and to tell you just how much you mean to me, that's all."

As he embraced Morgan, almost lifting her off the ground, the corner of his eye worked its way back to the activities inside and the servants doing their work. The couple lingered there for a while. They could see the final preparations being completed. Jean Toussaint, the three-star chef that Millie had bought from 'Le Pan' in New Orleans, was putting the finishing touches on the garnishments. He could see it all from the patio.

The Chef had created a portrait of Baker in his micro appetizers. Tiny squares, triangles, and rectangles were put together from the fractured geometry of Millie's insanity. These assholes would soon eat his face. But as sickening as that was to Baker, even that wasn't enough to distract him from something else.

The guests arrived and Morgan again latched on to Baker, dragging him back into the reception area. His resistance was minor, but her growing concern wasn't.

Baker watched carefully as Millie somehow kept herself going. Her unstoppable will to kill the weak must have been the force that pushed her forward. Morgan glowed with admiration as she watched her mother insult her servants, kiss her guests, and drink champagne.

Somehow, Baker kept himself and Morgan in a dark corner toward the back of the room. He even bent over and whispered to Morgan that he didn't want to take away the spotlight from Marvin and his speech to the guests. He told her it was Marvin's time to shine, not theirs, and that they could take their bow from anywhere in the room.

Maria Carmona, a recently hired maid and housekeeper, had won a slight bit of favor from Millie by her friendly and efficient demeanor. She did whatever Millie asked her to do, quietly and with respect. As a result, Millie honored her with the delicate task of handing out the glasses of champagne for toasting the engagement announcement. As the room filled, Marvin stood up, ready to make the big announcement to the guests.

Maria did her part, moving nimbly between the guests, holding the tray in perfect balance. Hips and elbows moved around her as she did her best to keep the drinks balanced on the tray she held high above her. It worked well until one guest bumped into her from behind, causing the glasses and the champagne to come crashing down, spilling on one of the guest's expensive evening dresses.

Millie saw the incident from across the room. Baker's pallor returned, along with his temporary suspension of disbelief. With both of her arms extended, Millie grabbed Maria away from the guest she was attempting to clean. "Keep your hands off my guests, you filthy little wetback," said Millie.

As she manhandled the shocked maid, the little gold locket Maria always wore fell to the ground. The clusters of wealth wanted more. Now the party was getting exciting. Maria didn't understand what was happening. As she picked herself up from the floor, the crowd edged closer. "Get up, bitch," said Millie. The crowd moved closer as they wanted more. Baker clenched his jaw.

As she got up to her feet, Maria stood in front of Millie and didn't move a muscle. Instead, she stared into Millie's eyes and, without the slightest hesitation, Millie slapped Maria across her face.

Morgan couldn't stop laughing as she watched her mother's anger foment into a whole new insanity. The little groups still edged in closer to the scene with their giggles becoming cackles. Maria's stoic face was now transformed.

Baker threw his drink down, smashing the glass as he ran to Maria. He could no longer think. His six-foot-four-inch frame got him to the scene in four giant strides, knocking down anyone in his way. Silence now filled the room.

He stood between Millie and Maria and asked Maria if she was ok. Something happened to her as she looked up at the tall figure in front of her. Baker spun himself around and glared down at the drunk.

"Apologize to this lady, right now Millie, and I mean right now."

"Apologize for what?"

"For this!" Baker slapped the drunk. Her numb skull thudded on the ornate Italian tile.

"Get up Millie," said Baker. The look on his face made her feel he was getting ready to hit her again when a couple of men in the crowd attempted to restrain him. He composed himself and the incident was over. He put his arm around Maria and escorted her away, pushing his way through the crowd and making a point of walking past Morgan, who couldn't believe what she was seeing. She stared at Baker as she ran to help her mother.

Baker left with Maria and Morgan, and Marvin lifted Millie. The spectators exited the arena as Millie begged them to stay. Then, one of them stepped on Maria's locket, opening it up for the world to see.

They left like a tide, leaving the shore and washing everything out with it. Millie cried to the tide as Marvin held the weeping Morgan in his arms. But tides come and go, even in The Hamptons.

No one noticed the broken locket on the floor or the picture of Maria with her son, now known as Baker James, at least for now, or the inscription on it that read: 'With all my love, Carlos, your loving son.'

ACKNOWLEDGEMENTS

The following stories have been previously published under my alter ego "Bennie Rosa": "Are We a Thing" in *us/them anthology*; "Dead Husband Money" in *The Charleston Anvil*; "Far Cries" in *Daddy a Cultural Anthology*; "Microboy Never Loved Christina" in *New World Writing* and in *Scarlett Leaf Review*; "The Rest" in *Barrio Beat*; "The Anniversary Party" (Previously titled "The Closer the Dawn") in *The Writer's Club*; "The Migrants: A Photo Album" in *IHRAF*; "The Many Apologies of Orville Carmody" in *The Writer's Club*; "Music for Simana" (Previously titled "The Guardian") in *IHRAF*.

Thank you for reading this book. If you're interested in learning more about the author or exploring additional resources related to this work, please visit the author's website at:

https://andy-slade.com

Don't miss out!

Visit the website below and you can sign up to receive emails whenever Andy Slade publishes a new book. There's no charge and no obligation.

https://books2read.com/r/B-A-SZBX-QHMPC

BOOKS 2 READ

Connecting independent readers to independent writers.

Did you love *Our Shadows Never Die*? Then you should read *Betrayal Is Beautiful*[1] by Andy Slade!

²

When an MIA Iraq War vet, John Chayne, is discovered in upstate New York, he decides to go to his home on a pueblo in Northwest New Mexico, only to find out that all hell has broken loose there. It has been taken over by a drug cartel and someone out of his past. The battle between his love for his native home, his family, and his own conscience almost destroys him and everyone around him.

---

1. https://books2read.com/u/bxr5Qo

2. https://books2read.com/u/bxr5Qo

Also by Andy Slade

Betrayal Is Beautiful
Our Shadows Never Die

About the Author

Andy Slade was born and raised in Brooklyn, New York, a place where dreams always seem real. He lived in San Francisco, a paradise for dreamers, especially for those who love to write stories. And with many stops along the way, he now lives in New Mexico, where the glowing sun inspires, and the spirit grows. *Betrayal is Beautiful* is Andy's first novel. It is set in The Land of Enchantment.

    Note: Andy Slade creates a path to freedom by never giving up. He guides the reader on a journey like his own. His varied experiences in life, including teaching and driving a NYC taxi among many others, give his stories a unique perspective that always keeps you on the edge of your seat with plot twists and surprises